The O'Sullivan Twins

Second in Enid Blyton's exciting
St. Clare's School series

Dragon
Grafton Books
A Division of the Collins Publishing Group
8 Grafton Street, London W1X 3LA

Published by Dragon Books 1967
Reprinted 1968, 1969, 1970, 1971, 1972, 1973, 1974,
1975 (twice), 1976, 1977, 1978, 1979, 1980 (twice), 1981,
1983, 1984, 1985 (twice)

First published in Great Britain by
Methuen & Co Ltd 1942

ISBN 0-583-30033-2

Printed and bound in Great Britain by
Collins, Glasgow

Set in Times

Enid Blyton

The O'Sullivan Twins

Text illustrations by Jenny Chapple

DRAGON
GRAFTON BOOKS
A Division of the Collins Publishing Group

LONDON GLASGOW
TORONTO SYDNEY AUCKLAND

Rita pushed Alison out of the way

"Mother! Did you know that Cousin Alison, who was at Redroofs School with us, is going to St. Clare's next term?" said Pat O'Sullivan, looking up from a letter she was reading. Her twin, Isabel, was reading it too, the two dark heads side by side at the breakfast table.

"Yes, I knew," said their mother, smiling. "Your Aunt Sarah wrote and told me. When she heard how much you liked St. Clare's, she decided to send Alison there too – and you can look after her a little, the first term."

"Alison is a bit stuck-up," said Pat. "We saw her these hols., Mummy – full of airs and graces. And she has had her hair permed – think of that!"

"Shocking! At her age!" said Mrs. O'Sullivan. "Quite time she went to St. Clare's!"

"I remember two girls who were terribly stuck-up last summer holidays," said Mr. O'Sullivan, looking up from his newspaper. His eyes twinkled as he looked at the twins. "My goodness – *they* didn't want to go to St. Clare's! They thought it would be a dreadful school – really horrid."

Pat and Isabel went very red. "Don't remind us of that, Daddy," said Pat. "We were idiots. We behaved awfully badly at St. Clare's at first – every one called us the Stuck-Up twins."

"Or the High-and-Mighties!" said Isabel, with a giggle. "Gracious – I can't think how any one put up with us."

"Well, we had a pretty bad time to start with," said

Pat. "And serve us right too. I hope Alison won't be as stuck-up as we were."

"She'll be worse," said Isabel. "She's so vain! Mummy, couldn't you get Alison to come and stay here for two or three days before we have to go back to St. Clare's? Then we could tell her a few things."

"Well, that would be very kind of you," said Mrs. O'Sullivan.

"It's not *alto*gether kindness," said Isabel, with a smile. "Neither Pat nor I want to be saddled with a cousin who's going to be silly and vain – and we may be able to prepare her a bit if we have her a few days."

"Lick her into shape, you mean?" said Mr. O'Sullivan, over the top of his paper. "Well, if you can make that conceited little monkey into somebody nice, I shall be surprised. I never saw any one so spoilt in all my life."

"It's a good thing she's going to St. Clare's," said Pat, spreading marmalade on her toast. "Don't you think Isabel and I are nicer since we went there, Daddy?"

"I'll have to think a little about that," said their father, teasingly. "Well – yes – on the whole I'm pleased with you. What do you say, Mother?"

"Oh, I think they settled down very well indeed at St. Clare's," said Mrs. O'Sullivan. "They did so hate going – and they vowed and declared they wouldn't try a bit – but Miss Theobald, the Head Mistress, said some very nice things on their report. They will be very happy there this term."

"I don't want the hols. to end, but I can't help feeling quite excited when I think of seeing old Mam'zelle Abominable again," said Pat, "and Miss Roberts, and . . ."

"Mam'zelle *Abominable*!" said Mr. O'Sullivan, in

astonishment. "Is that really her name?"

"Oh, no, Daddy — we only call her that because she says *'C'est abominable!'* to so many things!" said Pat. "Isabel and I were awfully bad at French grammar at first and Mam'zelle use to write 'Abominable' across our books. But she is a kind old thing, really."

"It will be fun to see all the girls again too," said Isabel. "Mummy, write and tell Aunt Sarah to let Cousin Alison come next week before we go back."

So Mrs. O'Sullivan wrote to her sister-in-law and Cousin Alison arrived two days before the girls were due back at school

She was a very pretty girl, with curled red-brown hair, a rose-bud mouth, and big blue eyes.

"A bit like that doll we used to have, really," said Pat to Isabel. "We called her Angela, do you remember? I wish Alison wouldn't smile that silly smile so much."

"Oh, I expect some one has told her what a sweet smile she has, or something," said Isabel. "Really she seems to think she's a film-star, the way she behaves!"

Alison was pleased to be with her cousins so that she might go to St. Clare's with them, for, like most girls, she felt nervous at going for the first time to a new school. It didn't take long to settle down — but it felt rather strange and new at first.

"Tell me a bit about the school," she said, as she sat down in the old schoolroom that evening. "I hope it isn't one of these terribly sensible schools that make you play games if you don't want to, and all that."

Pat winked at Isabel. "Alison, St. Clare's is just about the most sensible school in the kingdom!" she said, in a solemn voice. "You have to know how to clean shoes . . ."

7

"And make tea . . ." said Isabel.

"And toast," went on Pat. "And you have to know how to make your own beds . . ."

"And if you tear your clothes you have to mend them yourself," said Isabel, enjoying Alison's look of horror.

"Wait a minute," said Alison, sitting up. "What do you mean – clean shoes, make tea – and toast? Surely you don't do that!"

The twins laughed. "It's all right," said Pat. "You see, Alison, the first form and second form have to wait on the top-formers in turn. When they shout for us we have to go and see what they want, and jolly well do it."

Alison went pink. "It sounds pretty awful to me," she said. "What are the girls like? Are they awful too?"

"Oh, dreadful," said Pat, solemnly. "Very like Isabel and me, in fact. You'll probably hate them!"

"It doesn't sound a bit like Redroofs, the school you went to with me only a term ago," said Alison, sadly. "What's our form-mistress like? Shall I be in the same form as you?"

"Yes, I should think so," said Pat. "We are in the first form – we certainly shan't be moved up into the second yet. Our form-mistress is Miss Roberts. She's a good sort – but my word, she's sarcastic! If you get the wrong side of her you'll be sorry."

"And Mam'zelle is hot stuff too," said Isabel. "She's big, with enormous feet – and she's got a fearful temper and she shouts."

"Isabel, she sounds dreadful," said Alison, in alarm, thinking of the mouse-like French mistress at Redroofs.

"Oh, she's not a bad sort really," said Pat, smiling. "She's got a kind heart. Anyway, you needn't worry,

8

Alison – you'll have Isabel and me to look after you a bit and show you everything."

"Thanks," said Alison, gratefully. "I hope I'm in the same dormitory as you are. What's Matron like?"

"Oh, Matron has been there for years and years and years," said Pat. "She dosed our mothers and aunts, and our grandmothers too, for all I know? She knows when we've had Midnight Feasts – she doesn't stand any nonsense at all. But she's nice when you're ill."

Alison learnt a great deal about St. Clare's during the two days she stayed with the twins. She thought they had changed since they had left Redroofs. She stared at them and tried to think how they had changed.

"They seem so sensible," she thought. "They were always rather up in the air and proud, at Redroofs. Oh well – they were head-girls there, and had something to be proud of – now I suppose they're among the youngest in the school – and I shall be too."

The day came for the three to leave for their boarding-school. Everything had been packed. Mrs. O'Sullivan had got the same cakes and sweets for Alison's tuck-box as she had bought for the twins. Everything was neatly marked and well-packed, and now the three big trunks and the three tuck-boxes stood ready in the hall, marked in white paint with the names of the three girls.

Mrs. O'Sullivan was to see them off in London. Pat and Isabel were excited at the thought of seeing all their friends again. Alison was rather quiet. She was very glad that she had the twins to go with.

They arrived on the platform from which their train was to go – and then what an excitement there was! "There's dear old Janet! Hie, Janet, Janet! Did you have good hols.? Oh, there's Hilary. Hallo, Hilary –

9

look, this is our Cousin Alison who's coming to St. Clare's this term. Oh, there's Doris – and Sheila!"

Every one crowded round the twins, talking and laughing. Alison was made known to them all, and she felt very grateful to the twins for helping her in this difficult first meeting with unknown girls.

A pleasant-faced mistress bustled up with a note-book in hand. "Good morning, Pat, good morning, Isabel! Still as like as two peas, I see! Is this your cousin, Alison O'Sullivan? Good – I'll tick her off in my list. How do you do, Alison? I'm Miss Roberts, your form-mistress. No doubt the twins have told you exactly how fierce and savage I am!"

She smiled and passed on to the next group. It was her job to see that all the first- and second-formers were there, and to get them into the train in time.

"Any new girls this term?" wondered Pat, looking round. "I can't see any – except Alison, of course."

"Yes – there's one over there – look!" said Isabel, nudging Pat. Pat looked, and saw a tall, rather good-looking girl standing by herself. She had a bad-tempered face, and was not trying to make friends with anyone at all. No one had come to see her off.

"*She's* new," said Pat. "I wonder if she'll be in our form. My word, I should think she's got a temper – I wonder what would happen if she and Janet had a row!"

Janet was very quick-tempered, and flared up easily. But it was soon over with her; this new girl, however, looked sulky, as well as bad tempered. The twins did not take to her at all.

"There's another new girl, too – look, just walking on to the platform!" said Isabel. "She looks jolly nice! She'll be in our form, I should think."

The second new girl was quite different from the one they had just seen. She was small, with dancing black curls, and she had deep blue eyes that sparkled and shone. Her father and mother were both with her.

"Her father must be an artist or a musician or something, his hair's so long!" said Pat.

"*I know* who he is," said Hilary Wentworth, who was standing just nearby. "He's Max Oriell – the famous painter. My aunt has just had her portrait painted by him – it's simply marvellous. I saw him one or twice when I went with her to a sitting. That must be his daughter. They're awfully alike."

"She looks clever," said Pat. "I hope she's in our form."

"Get into your carriages, please!" called Miss Roberts, in her clear voice. "The train goes in three minutes. Say your good-byes now."

So good-byes were said and the girls scrambled into their carriages, trying to sit by their own special friends. Alison thought that the top-formers, walking sedately along the platform, were very grown-up and dignified. She felt small when she saw them.

"There's Winifred James, our head girl," whispered Pat, as a tall, serious-looking girl went by. "She's frightfully clever, and most awfully nice."

"I should be afraid to say a word to her!" said Alison.

"We felt like that at first too," said Isabel. "Look – that's Belinda Towers, the sports captain. Pat and I got into a row with her last term – but we soon found she was a good sort. Golly, I hope she puts us down for a few matches this term, don't you, Pat?"

The whistle blew. Handkerchiefs waved from windows. The train puffed out slowly, full to bursting-point with all the girls of St. Clare's. They were off to school again!

The first day or two of a new term is always an exciting time. There are no proper time-tables, rules are not kept strictly, there is a lot of unpacking to be done – and best of all there are tuck-boxes to empty!

The twins missed their home and their mother at first, as did most girls – but there was so much to do that there was no time to fret or worry. In any case every one soon settled down into the school routine. It was fun to greet all the teachers again, fun to sit in the same old classroom, and fun to see if the ink-spot that looked like a cat with two tails was still on Janet's desk.

There were new books to be given out, and new pencils, rubbers, rulers and pens.

"Ah, the nice new books!" said Mam'zelle, her large eyes gleaming with pleasure as she looked round the class. "The nice new books – to be filled with beautiful French compositions. Did you groan, Doris? Surely you are not going to make my hair grey this term as you did last term? Ah-h-h! See this grey lock, *ma chère* Doris – it was you who caused that last term!"

Mam'zelle pulled out a bit of grey hair from her thick thatch, and looked comically at Doris.

"I'll do my best, Mam'zelle," promised Doris. "But I shall never, never be able to say the French r's in the right way. Never!"

"R-r-r-r!" said Mam'zelle, rolling the r in her throat in a most marvellous manner. The class giggled. Mam'zelle sounded remarkably like a dog growling, but nobody dared to say so.

The other teachers welcomed the girls in their own

manner. Miss Roberts had already seen most of her girls in the train. Alison couldn't help liking her very much, though she was a little afraid of Miss Roberts's sharp tongue. Miss Roberts had a way of making an offender feel very small indeed.

The form-mistress had a special word for the twins. "Well, Pat and Isabel, I can see by your faces that you've made up your minds to do well this term. You've got determination written all over you, Pat – and I know that Isabel always follows your example! What about being top in a few things this term?"

"I'd like to be," said Pat, eagerly. "We always were at Redroofs – the school we went to before, you know. Now that we've got used to St. Clare's we'll be able to work more quickly."

Matron was in her room, giving out towels, sheets and pillow-cases, and warning everyone that any buttons would have to be sewn on by the girls themselves, and any tears would have to be neatly mended in sewing-class.

"But I can't mend sheets and things," said Alison, in dismay.

"Maybe that's one of the things your mother sent you here to learn?" suggested Matron with her wide smile. "You hope to be happily married one day, don't you – and run your own home? Well, you must learn to take care of your own linen and mend it, then. But it doesn't seem to me that you need worry much – your mother has sent you all new things. So unless you *try* to kick holes in your sheets, and tear the buttons off there won't be much for you to do in the way of mending *this* term!"

All the girls had to go and see Miss Theobald in turn. Alison went with Pat and Isabel. She felt very

13

nervous as she stood outside the drawing-room with them, waiting to go in.

"What do I *say*?" she whispered. "Is she very solemn?"

The door opened and Janet and Hilary came out. "You next," said Hilary, and the waiting three went in. Alison liked Miss Theobald, the Head Mistress, at once. She had a very serious face that could break into a really lovely smile. She smiled now as she saw the three cousins.

"Well, Pat and Isabel, I am glad to see you back again, looking so happy," she said. "I remember last term, when I first saw you, you scowled and said hardly a word! But this term I know you better. You will do your very best for your form, and for the school too."

"Yes, of course, Miss Theobald," said the twins, beaming.

Miss Theobald turned to Alison. "And this is another O'Sullivan, a cousin!" she said. "Well, with three O'Sullivans all working hard in the same form, Miss Roberts ought to be pleased! You are lucky to have two sensible cousins to help you along in this first term, Alison."

"Yes, Miss Theobald," gasped Alison, still very nervous.

"You may go now," said Miss Theobald. "And remember, Pat and Isabel, that I am here to help in any difficulty, so don't be afraid to come, will you?"

The three went out, all a little awed, but all liking the Head Mistress immensely. They rushed to the common room, which Alison had not yet seen.

"Don't we have studies to ourselves here?" said Alison, in disappointment, looking round the big room that was shared by the first- and second-formers together. "What an awful row!"

Certainly there was a noise. Girls were talking and laughing. Some one had put the gramophone on, and some one else, at the other end of the big room, was tinkering with the wireless, which kept making most extraordinary noises.

"You'll soon get used to the noise," said Pat happily. "It's nice and friendly, really. Look – you can have this part of the shelf here for your belongings, Alison – your cake-tins and biscuit-tins – and your sewing or knitting and the library book you're reading. The next part belongs to me and Isabel. Keep your part tidy or you'll take up too much room."

The twins showed their cousin over the school – the big classrooms with the lovely view from the windows – the enormous gym – the fine art room, high-up under the roof, with a good north light – the laboratory – even the cloakrooms, where each girl had a locker for her shoes, and a peg for her out-door things and her overall.

"Am I in the same dormitory as you, Pat?" asked Alison, timidly, as she peeped in at the big bedrooms, where eight girls slept in eight little cubicles each night.

"I'll ask Hilary," said Pat. "She's head-girl of our form, and she'll know. Hie, Hilary – do you know if our Cousin Alison is in with us, or not?"

Hilary took out a list of names. "Dormitory 8," she read out. "Hilary Wentworth, Pat and Isabel O'Sullivan, Doris Elward, Kathleen Gregory, Shelia Naylor, Janet Robins and Alison O'Sullivan. There you are – that's our dormitory list – same as last term, except that Vera Johns has gone into number 9 – to make room for Alison, I suppose."

15

"Oh, good," said Pat. "You're with us, Alison. That's a bit of luck for you."

The three new girls were in the first form with Miss Roberts. The tall bad-tempered-looking girl was called Margery Fenworthy. She looked old enough to be in the second form, but the girls soon saw that her work was poor – not even up to the standard of the first form, really.

"Isn't she a funny creature?" said Pat to Isabel, after a morning in class with Margery. "She simply doesn't seem to care a bit what she does or says. I've an idea she can be awfully rude. Goodness – there'll be a row if she gets across Mam'zelle!"

Margery Fenworthy kept herself to herself. She was always reading, and if anyone spoke to her she answered so shortly that nobody said any more. She would have been very good looking if she had smiled – but, as Pat said, she always looked as if she wanted to bite somebody's head off!

Lucy Oriell, the other new girl, was the complete opposite of Margery. She was brilliantly clever, but as she was only fourteen and a half, she was put into the first form for that term at any rate. Nothing was difficult to her. She had a wonderful memory, and was always merry and gay.

"The way she gabbles French with Mam'zelle!" groaned Doris. "The way she draws in the art class! The way she recites yards and yards of Shakespeare, and it takes me all my time to learn two lines properly."

Every one laughed. Doris was a duffer – with one great talent. She could make people laugh! She could dance well and comically, and she could mimic others perfectly, which made it all the more strange that she could not imitate Mam'zelle's French accent. Every one liked Doris.

16

"An absolute idiot – but such a nice one!" as Janet said.

"What do you think of the three new girls, Janet?" asked Hilary, biting the end of her pencil as she tried to think out a problem in arithmetic set by Miss Roberts.

Pat and Isabel were nearby, listening. Janet shook back her dark hair, and gave her judgment.

"Lucy Oriell – top-hole! Clever, responsible, kind and gay. Margery Fenworthy – a bad-tempered, don't-care creature with some sort of PAST."

"Whatever do you mean?" said Pat, astonished.

"Well, mark my words, there's something behind that funny way Margery has of keeping herself to herself, and of not caring tuppence for anything or anybody," said Janet, who could be very far-seeing when she wanted to. "And what does a girl of fifteen want to be so bad-tempered for? I'd just like to know how she got on at her last school. I bet she didn't make any friends!"

The twins stared across at Margery, who, as usual, had her nose buried in a book. Janet went on to the third new girl, Alison.

"I suppose I mustn't say much about Alison, as she's your cousin – but if you want my real opinion it's this – she's a conceited, stuck-up little monkey without a single idea in her pretty little head!"

"Thanks for your opinions, Janet," said Hilary, with a laugh. "You have a wonderful way of putting into words just exactly what every one else is thinking – and doesn't say!"

The Easter term opened very cold and dreary. The girls shivered when they got up in the morning. Alison simply hated getting up. Time after time Hilary stripped the clothes from her, and Alison almost wept with anger. Nothing like that had ever happened at her old school!

"Don't do that!" she cried, each time. "I was *just* going to get up!"

Every one grinned. They thought Alison was very silly sometimes. She spent ages doing her hair and looking at herself in the glass – and if she had a spot on her face she moaned about it for days till it went.

"As if anybody would notice if she had twenty spots!" said Janet, in disgust. "She's not worth looking at, the vain little thing!"

In a week or two it seemed to the twins as if they had been back at school for months! Each form was now working steadily to its own time-table. Lacrosse games were played three times a week, and any one could go to the field and practise in their spare time. Gym was held twice a week, and the twins loved that. The new girl, Margery, was excellent at all the things they did in gym.

"She's strong, isn't she?" said Pat, admiringly, as they watched her climbing up the thick rope that hung down from the ceiling.

"She plays games and does gym as if she was fighting somebody fiercely all the time!" said Janet, hitting the nail on the head, as usual. "Look at her grit-

18

ting her teeth as she climbs that rope. My word, I don't like marking her at lacrosse I can tell you. She's given me some bruises across my knuckles even though I wear padded gloves!"

Janet showed the bruises. "She's a savage creature!" said Doris. "Belinda ticked her off yesterday for deliberately tripping me up on the field. All the same, she'd be a good one to have in a match! If she wanted to shoot a goal she'd jolly well shoot one, even if she had to knock down every single one of the other side!"

Lucy Oriell was a fine lacrosse player too. She had been captain of the lacrosse team at her old school, and she was as swift as the wind.

"She's good at everything, the lucky creature!" said Hilary. "Have you seen some of her pictures? They really are lovely. She showed me some water-colours she'd done in the hols. with her father. I couldn't believe they were hers. Of course, she gets that from him. He must make a lot of money from his portraits – no wonder all her dresses are so good."

"It's a pity that silly cousin of yours doesn't try a bit harder at games," said Janet, watching Alison trying to catch a lacrosse ball in her net. It was a very easy throw sent by Kathleen. But Alison muffed it as usual.

"Alison, haven't you ever played games before?" cried Janet.

"Yes," said Alison, flushing. "But I played hockey – much better game than this stupid lacrosse. I'd always rather hit a ball than catch it! I was jolly good at hockey, wasn't I, Pat, at Redroofs?"

Pat did not remember Alison ever being any good at any game, so she said nothing. Belinda Towers came up and spoke to the twins.

"I say, can't you do something about that silly little

19

cousin of yours? She just stands and bleats at me when I order her to practise catching and throwing! She wants a bit of pep in her."

Pat laughed. Alison did bleat – that was just the right word for it.

"I'll try and take her in hand," she said. "After all, I was pretty awful myself at first, last term – and I'll try and knock some sense into Alison, in the same way that it was knocked into me and Isabel."

"She thinks too much about herself," said Belinda, in her direct way. "Stupid sickly smile, big blue eyes, bleating little voice – make her skip round a bit, can't you? I really can't stand much more of her."

So Pat and Isabel made Alison skip around a bit! She was very indignant indeed.

"Why do you always make me go and practise this silly catching just when I want to finish my book!" she grumbled. "Why do you hustle me out for a walk when it's so cold and windy? If you call this looking after me I'd rather you stopped!"

Soon it was Alison's turn to wait on the two top-formers, Rita George and Katie White! They sent a runner for her at tea-time one day. Alison had just finished her own tea when the message came.

"Alison! Rita wants you. Buck up. It's your turn to do her jobs this week."

"What jobs?" said Alison, crossly, swallowing her last mouthful of cake.

"How do I know? Making her tea, I expect. And I think the fire's gone out in her room. You'll have to rake it out and lay it again for her."

Alison nearly burst with indignation. "What, me light a fire! I've never lighted one in my life! I don't even know how to lay one."

"If you don't go, Alison, you'll get into a row," said

Isabel. "Katie White isn't as patient as Rita. Go on. Don't be a ninny."

Alison, grumbling under her breath all the while, went slowly off to Rita's study. Rita looked up impatiently as she came in.

"Good heavens, are you always as slow as this! What bad luck to have *you* waiting on us this week. We won't get a thing done!"

"Rake out the fire and lay it again quickly," said Katie White, in her deep voice. "There's some paper and sticks in that cupboard. Go on, now – we've got some other girls coming in for tea."

Poor Alison! She raked out the fire as best she could, got the paper and sticks from the cupboard and put them higgledy-piggledy into the grate. The grate was hot and she burnt her hand when she touched it. She let out a loud squeal.

"What's the matter?" said Rita, startled.

"I've burnt my hand on the hot grate," said Alison, nursing her hand against her chest, though really it hardly hurt at all.

"Well, really – did you imagine the grate would be stone-cold after having had a fire in it all day?" asked Rita, impatiently. "For goodness' sake hurry up and light the fire. There's a box of matches on the mantelpiece."

Alison took down the matches. She struck one and held it to the paper; it flared up at once. At the same moment three more big girls came in, chattering. One was Belinda Towers. No one took any notice of the first-former lighting the fire. Alison felt very small and unimportant.

The paper burnt all away. The sticks of wood did not catch alight at all. Bother! There was no more paper in the cupboard. Alison turned timidly to Rita.

21

"Please, where is there some more paper?"

"On the desk over there," said Rita, shortly, scowling at Alison. The top-formers went on talking and Alison went to a nearby desk. She looked at the papers there. They were sheets covered with Rita's small neat hand-writing.

"I suppose it's old work she doesn't want," thought Alison, and picked it up. She arranged the sheets in the fire-place, and then set a match to them. At the same moment she heard a loud exclamation from Rita.

"I say! I say! You surely haven't taken my prep. to burn? She has! Oh, the silly donkey, she's taken my French prep.!"

There was a rush for the fire. Alison was pushed out of the way. Rita tried to pull some of the blazing sheets out – but the flames had got a good hold of them and she could not save any of her precious prep. It was burnt to black ashes.

"Alison! How dare you do a thing like that," cried Rita, in a rage. "You deserve to have your ears boxed."

"I didn't mean to," said poor Alison, beginning to cry all over the fire-place, near which she was still kneeling. "You said – take the paper on the desk over there – and . . ."

"Well, can't you tell the difference between yesterday's newspaper and to-day's French prep.?" stormed the angry fifth-former. "Now I shall have to do an hour's extra work and rewrite all that French!"

"*And* she hasn't even lighted the fire yet!" said Belinda Towers. "Just as stupid at doing household jobs as you are in the sports field, Alison."

"Please let me go," wept Alison, feeling half-dead with shame before the accusing faces of the big girls. "I can't light a fire. I really can't."

"Then it's just about time you learnt," said Rita,

grimly. "No, where's that paper? Put it like this – and like this. Now get the sticks. Arrange them so that the flames can lick up them and set the coal alight. Now put some coal on the top. Good heavens, idiot, what's the good of putting an enormous lump like that on top? You've squashed down all the sticks! Take little lumps to start a fire with – like this."

Alison wept all the time, feeling terribly sorry for herself. She held a match to the paper with a shaking hand. It flared up – the sticks caught – the coal burnt – and there was the fire, burning merrily.

"Now put the kettle on the hob just there, and you can go, baby," said Katie. "Where do you get all those tears from? For goodness' sake, come away from the fire or you'll put it out again!"

Alison crept out of the room, tears running down her cheeks. She stopped at a mirror and looked at herself. She thought that she looked a most sad pathetic sight – rather like a film-star she had seen crying in a picture. She went back to the common room, sniffing, hoping that every one would sympathize with her.

But to her surprise, nobody did – not even kind-hearted Lucy Oriell. Pat looked up and asked her what was up.

Alison told her tale. When she related how she had burnt Rita's French prep. papers the first-formers looked horrified.

"Fathead!" said Janet, in disgust. "Letting down our form like that! Golly, the big girls must think we are mutton-heads!"

"It was *awful* being rowed at by so many of the big girls," wept Alison, thinking that she must look a very pathetic sight. But every one was disgusted.

"Stop it, Alison. You're not in a kindergarten," said Hilary. "If you want to behave like an idiot, you must

23

expect the top-formers to treat you like one. For goodness' sake stop sniffing. You look simply awful, I can tell you. Your eyes are red, your nose is swollen, your mouth has gone funny – you look just as ugly as can be!"

That made Alison weep really bitterly. Janet lost her temper. "Either stop, or go out," she said roughly to Alison. "If you don't stop I'll put you out of the room myself. You've no right to disturb us all like this."

Alison looked up. She saw that sharp-tongued Janet meant what she said. So she stopped crying at once, and the twins grinned at each other.

"Lesson number one!" whispered Pat.

Tessie has a Secret

The first real excitement of the term was Tessie's birthday. Tessie was a lively girl in the second form, fond of tricks and jokes. She and Janet were a pair! The girls often laughed when they remembered how the term before Janet had thrown fire-works on the schoolroom fire, and given poor Miss Kennedy such a fright.

"And do you remember how Tessie hid the big black cat in the handwork cupboard, and it jumped out at Miss Kennedy and made her rush out of the room?" giggled Doris. "Oh, golly – I've never laughed so much in all my life."

Miss Kennedy had gone, and in her place was Miss Lewis, a first-class history-teacher. The girls liked her very much, except for one thing – she would not allow the slightest inattention or cheekiness in her classes. Even free-tongued Janet was a model of good behaviour in Miss Lewis's classes. Only surly Margery seemed to care nothing for anything the history teacher said.

Tessie had great ideas for her birthday. She knew she would have plenty of money sent to her, and plenty of good things to eat. She was a generous girl, and wanted every one to share.

But there would not be enough for every one. If Tessie put all her things on the table at tea-time there would only be a tiny bit for each of the forty or fifty first- and second-formers.

Tessie thought about it. She talked to her great friend, Winnie Thomas.

"Winnie, don't you think it would be better to share my things amongst a few of my *best* friends – and not give every one only a taste?" said Tessie.

"Yes, I do think that," said Winnie. "But when can we give the party? We can't very well just ask a few of the ones we like, and leave the rest to stare jealously!"

"Well, we'll have to have the party when there's no one there except the ones we ask," said Tessie. "And that means – at night! On my birthday night!"

"But we can't have it in the dormitory," said Winnie. "The others would know then. We must keep it a secret. It won't be any fun if we don't."

"We won't have it in the dormitory," said Tessie. "But where in the world *can* we have it, without being found out?"

"I know! We'll have it in that little music-room not far from our dormitory!" said Winnie, her eyes shining. "It's just the place. No one ever goes there at night. If we pull down the blinds, and shut the door no one will ever know we are there. We mustn't make much noise though – it's rather near Mam'zelle's study."

25

"It'll be all the more fun if we mustn't make much noise," giggled Tessie. "How can we warm that room? It's awfully cold in there. I know, becuse I had to practise there last week."

"Let's borrow an oil-stove out of the cupboard downstairs!" said Winnie. "Some of them have oil in, I know, because they're not emptied when they are put away in that cupboard."

"Good idea!" said Tessie, who liked everything to be as perfect as possible when she planned anything. Then a thought struck her – "Oooh, Winnie – do you think we could fry sausages on top of the oil-stove if I could buy some? I could get some of those tiny little sausages – I forget what they're called – the kind people often have to put round chickens?"

Winnie stared at Tessie in delight. "I don't believe ANY ONE has ever fried sausages at a birthday party in the middle of the night before!" she said. "Not any one. It would be a most marvellous thing to do. Can we get a frying-pan?"

"You bet!" said Tessie. "I'll ask young Gladys, the scullery-maid, to lend me one for the night. She's a good sport and won't tell. And if I can't borrow one, I'll jolly well buy one!"

"Tessie, this is going to be awful fun," said Winnie, dancing about. "What do you suppose you'll have for your party – besides your birthday cake and the sausages?"

"Well, Mother always sends me a big fruit cake, a ginger cake, sweets, biscuits and home-made toffee," said Tessie. "And I'll have plenty of money to buy anything else we want. I'll get some tins of peaches. We all like those."

The two girls went into corners and whispered excitedly every day. Mam'zelle noticed their inattention in class and scolded them for it.

"Tessie! Winnie! Do you wish me to send you down into the first-form? You sit there staring out of the window and you do not pay one small piece of attention to all I am saying! What mischief are you planning?"

This was so near the mark that both girls went red. "It's my birthday soon, Mam'zelle," said Tessie, meekly, knowing that Mam'zelle usually understood an excuse like that.

"Ah, I see – and I suppose it is dear Winnie's birthday also?" said Mam'zelle. "Well, unless you both wish to write me out a ver-r-r-ry nice composition in your best French all about birthdays you will please pay attention to *me*."

The two girls decided to ask only six more girls to the party. Tessie didn't see why they should all be from the second-form. "You know, I like those O'Sullivan twins awfully," she said. "I'd like to ask them. They're good sports."

"Yes – but for goodness' sake don't ask that awful cousin of theirs, always strutting about like a peacock," said Winnie.

"Of course not," said Tessie. "I simply couldn't bear her. No – we'll ask Pat and Isabel – and Janet. And out of our own form we'll ask Hetty, Susan and Nora. What do you think of that?"

"Yes – fine," agreed Winnie.

"We'll have to be careful not to let that sneaky Erica guess about our party," said Tessie, thoughtfully. "She's such a Paul-Pry – always sticking her nose into things that don't concern her. She's an awful tell-tale too. I'm sure she sneaked about me to Miss Jenks, when I lost that lacrosse ball."

27

"We'll tell every one to keep it a close secret," said Winnie. "I say – won't it be fun?"

Tessie got hold of the twins that day and took them to a corner. "Listen," she said, "I'm having a small birthday party on Thursday – just you and five others. Will you come?"

"Oh, yes, thanks," said Pat, pleased at being asked by a second-former.

"What time?" asked Isabel.

"Twelve o'clock at night," giggled Tessie. The twins stared in surprise.

"Oh – is it a midnight feast, like we had last term?" asked Pat, eagerly.

"No – not quite," said Tessie. "It's not going to be held in the dormitory, like a midnight feast – we are going to have it in that little music-room not far from my dormitory. You know the one I mean?"

"Yes," said Pat. "I say – what fun! It will be a proper midnight party, all by ourselves. Who else are you asking?"

"Four from my form, not counting myself," said Tessie, "and you two and Janet from your form. That's all. Now mind you come at twelve o'clock. And oh – I say!"

"What?" asked the twins.

"Don't say a word to any one, will you," begged Tessie. "You see, I can't ask every one, and some of the girls might be a bit annoyed they haven't been asked."

"Of course we won't say a word," said Pat. The twins went off together, and waited until Tessie had told Janet. Then the three of them whispered together excitedly about the twelve-o'clock party! It was fun to have a secret. It was fun to be asked by a second-former – chosen out of all the girls in their form!

28

Alison was very curious, for she knew quite well that her cousins had a secret. She kept badgering them to tell her.

"Oh, shut up, Alison," said Pat. "Can't we have a secret without telling the whole form?"

"It wouldn't be telling the whole form, if you only told *me*," said Alison, opening her blue eyes very wide and looking as beseeching as she could.

"My dear Alison, telling you would be quite the quickest way of telling the whole *school!*" said Pat. "You can't keep your mouth shut about anything. You just go round and bleat out every single thing."

This wasn't very kind but it was perfectly true. Alison couldn't keep anything to herself at all, and had so often given away little things that the twins had told her that now they left her out of all their secrets.

Alison went away, pouting. Erica, from the second form, saw her and went up to her. She was just as curious as Alison about other people's plans and secrets.

"It's a mean trick, to have plans and keep every one in the dark," said Erica. "I know Tessie and Winnie have got some sort of plan too – it's about Tessie's birthday, I think. I wish we could find out about it. That would just serve them right."

Alison didn't like Erica. Few people did, for she really was a sneak. Not even the mistresses liked her, for they much preferred not to know what was going on rather than have Erica come telling tales.

So Alison would not take Erica's hint and try to find out what was up, though she really longed to do so. Erica asked her again and again if she had discovered anything, but Alison stubbornly shook her head. Silly little vain thing as she was, she was not going to find out things to tell Erica.

Hetty, Susan and Nora kept their mouths shut too, about the party. Winnie, of course, did not say a word to any one except the four in her form who knew. So it was very difficult for Erica really to find out anything much. She guessed that it was to do with Tessie's birthday – and she guessed it was a party – but how, where and when she had no idea.

The plans went steadily forward. Gladys, the little scullery maid, giggled when Tessie asked her for the loan of a frying-pan. She put one under her apron and went to find Tessie. On the way she met Erica.

"Whatever are you hiding under your apron, Gladys?" said Erica, with the high and mighty air that the servants so much disliked. Gladys tossed her neat little head.

"Nothing to do with you, miss," she answered pertly. Erica was angry. She pulled Glady's apron aside and saw the pan.

"Oho! For Miss Tessie's party!" she said. It was only a guess – but Gladys at once thought Erica knew.

"Well, miss, if you knew, why did you ask me?" she said. "I'm to take it to the little music-room near Miss Tessie's dormitory."

Erica watched Gladys slip inside the music-room and put the pan into a cupboard, under a pile of music. It was Tessie's birthday today. So the party was near – probably at night. The inquisitive girl burned with curiosity and jealousy.

Tessie was having a marvellous birthday. She was a popular girl, for she was amusing and lively. The girls gave her small presents and wished her many happy returns of the day. Tessie handed round a big box of chocolates to every one in her form. Her grandmother had sent it for her – and Tessie meant to share

30

something with *all* her friends, even though she could not share her party with every one.

Erica kept as close as she could to Tessie and Winnie that day, hoping to find out something more about the party. She saw Tessie go to the cupboard where the oil-stoves were kept – and fetch out a big stove!

She did not dare to ask Tessie what she was doing with it, for Tessie had a sharp tongue for Erica. But she hid behind a door and watched Tessie through the crack.

Into the music-room went Tessie, carrying the heavy stove. Erica's eyes shone with delight. She felt sure that the party was to be held there. "It will have to be after eleven," thought the girl. "I know pretty well everything now – serves Tessie right for leaving me out! Nasty, sharp-tongued creature! I've a good mind to spoil the party!"

It is quite likely that Erica would have done nothing more, now that she was satisfied she knew the secret, if Winnie and Tessie had not caught her taking a chocolate from the big box that Tessie had handed round. Tessie had left it in her classroom, meaning to ask Miss Lewis, the history teacher, to have one. Erica had seen it there, and had not been able to stop herself from lifting the lid to look at the layers.

She could not resist taking one of the chocolates and popping it in to her mouth. After all, there were plenty! But just at that moment Tessie and Winnie came running into the room.

They stopped in amazement when they saw Erica hurriedly shutting the lid of the box. It was quite plain that she had a chocolate in her mouth.

"You are simply disgusting, Erica," said Tessie, coldly. "If you'd wanted another and had asked me I'd have willingly given you as many as you wanted.

31

But to sneak in and take one like that – you really are a disgusting creature."

The two girls went out. Erica had not been able to say a word. A chocolate was only a chocolate – how dared Tessie speak to her like that? Erica's cheeks burned and she longed to throw the whole box of sweets out of the window.

But she did not dare to. She went to her desk and slouched down into the seat. "Calling me disgusting!" said the girl, in a fury. "I won't have it! I'll pay her out for this! I'll spoil her precious party! I'll keep awake to-night till I see them going out of the dormitory – then I'll find a way to have them all caught!"

What Happened at the Party

Everything was ready for the party. Tessie had even been into the little music-room and lighted the oil-stove to get the room warm for her guests!

"No one ever goes in there at night," she said to Winnie, who was afraid that somebody might see the stove, if they went in. "The room will be lovely and warm by the time we are ready!"

The two girls were in a great state of excitement. Tessie had had *two* birthday cakes sent to her, which pleased her very much. She had been able to put the bigger one of the two on the tea-table for all her form to share – and had kept the other for the midnight party.

There were biscuits, sweets, chocolates, a big fruit cake, and four tins of peaches, with a tin of Nestle's milk for cream! There were also the strings of little sausages to fry. It was going to be great fun!

"We haven't anything to drink!" whispered Winnie to Tessie, in arithmetic at the end of that morning.

"Yes, we have. I've got some ginger-beer," whispered back Tessie. Miss Jenks caught the word "ginger-beer".

"Tessie, how does ginger-beer come into our arithmetic lesson?" she enquired, coldly.

"Well – it doesn't," said Tessie, at a loss what to say. "Sorry, Miss Jenks."

Susan, Hetty and Nora winked at one another. They knew quite well where the ginger-beer came in! Erica saw the winks and smiled to herself. She was going to spoil that party, ginger-beer and all!

Everything was hidden in the music-room, ready for that night. The eight girls were in a great state of excitement. They had all been in to peep at the things in the cupboard. The music-mistress would have been most surprised if she had taken a peep too – for instead of the usual piles of old music, a metronome or two, old hymn-books and so on, she would have seen a big birthday cake with "Happy returns to Tessie!" on it, and a big tin full of other goodies – to say nothing of eight fat brown ginger-beer bottles!

"How are we going to keep awake till twelve o'clock?" said Pat to Isabel and Janet.

"Oh, I'll be awake at twelve," said Janet, who had lately got the idea that she could wake at any time she liked, merely by repeating the hour to herself half a dozen times before she went to sleep. "I shall simply say 'twelve o'clock' firmly to myself before I go to sleep. And then I shall wake on the first stroke of midnight! You just see ."

"Well, Janet, I hope you're right," said Pat, doubtfully. "I've tried that heaps of times but it never works with me. I just go on sleeping."

Soon they were creeping down the stairs

"It's will-power," said Janet. "You needn't worry. I shall wake you all right!"

So the twins went peacefully to sleep as usual at half-past nine, trusting to Janet to wake them. Janet went to sleep too, saying 'twelve o'clock, twelve o'clock' steadily to herself, as she dropped off.

But alas for Janet! Midnight came – and she slept on! Her will-power must have been a little weak that night. The three first-formers would certainly have missed the party if the second-formers hadn't sent to see why they didn't turn up!

Pat was awakened by some one tugging at her arm, and a torch being flashed into her face. She woke with a jump and was just about to give a squeal of fright when she saw that it was Winnie who held the torch. In a flash she remembered the party.

"Pat! For goodness' sake! Aren't you three coming?" whispered Winnie.

"Of course," said Pat. "I'll wake the others." She threw off the bed-clothes, slipped her feet into her slippers and put on her warm dressing-gown. She went to wake Isabel and Janet. Soon the three of them were creeping out of the room, down a few stairs, round a corner past the second-form dormitory, and into the music-room.

The door opened and shut quietly and the three girls blinked at the bright electric light. The blinds had been drawn and the oil-stove had made the little room as warm as toast. The other five girls were busy opening tins and setting out cake and biscuits.

"Whatever happened to you?" said Tessie, in surprise. "It's a quarter-past twelve. We waited and waited. Then we sent Winnie."

"It was my fault," said Janet, looking ashamed of herself, a most unusual thing for Janet. "I promised

I'd wake them – and I didn't. I say – what a marvellous cake!"

The girls set to work to eat all the good things, giggling at nothing. It was so exciting to be cooped up in the little music-room, gobbling all sorts of goodies when every one else was fast asleep.

"Oh, Susan – you've spilt peach-juice all over my toes," giggled Janet.

"Lick it off then," said Susan. "I bet you can't!"

Janet was very supple. She at once tried to reach her foot up to her mouth to lick off the juice from her bare pink toes. She overbalanced and fell off her music-stool.

"Janet! You've sat on the sausages!" hissed Tessie, in dismay. "Get up, you idiot. Oh, the poor sausages – all squashed as flat as pan-cakes!"

The girls began to giggle helplessly. Tessie tried to press the little sausages back into their ordinary shape again.

"When are we going to fry them?" asked Isabel, who loved sausages.

"Last thing," said Tessie. "That is, if there is anything left of them when Janet has finished with them!"

The ginger-beer was opened. Each bottle had a top that had to be taken off with an opener, and each bottle gave a pop as it was opened.

"If any one hears these pops they'll wonder whatever's happening in this music-room," said Susan.

"Well, nobody *will* hear," said Tessie. "Every one is fast asleep. Not a soul in our own dormitory knows that we slipped out. Not a single person knows our secret!"

But Tessie boasted too soon. Some one was already outside the closed door, with her eye to the keyhole and her sharp ears trying to catch all that was said. Erica knew quite well all that was going on. Soon she caught her own name, and she stiffened outside the door, as she tried to hear what was said.

It was Tessie who was speaking. She was handing round the chocolates. "We caught that nasty little sneak Erica helping herself to the chocolates this afternoon," she said, in her clear voice. 'Isn't she the limit?"

"Oh, she's always doing things like that," said Pat. "You can't trust her an inch."

Erica felt the tears coming into her eyes. The girls had often told her unpleasant things to her face – but somehow it was horrible hearing them spoken behind her back. But the tears passed into tears of rage.

"I'll give them a few frights!" thought Erica, furiously. "And then I'll go and fetch Miss Jenks. It will serve the wretches right."

Erica knocked softly on the door, and then, quick as lightning, darted into a nearby cupboard. She hoped that her knocking would give the girls a shock.

It gave them a most terrible shock! They all stopped talking at once, and Tessie put down the box of chocolates with a shaking hand. They stared at one another, round-eyed.

"What was that?" whispered Tessie.

"A knock at the d-d-d-door," stuttered Winnie.

There was dead silence. Every one waited to see if the door would open. But it didn't.

Erica was still hidden in the cupboard. As nothing happened, she crept out again and knocked once more on the door, this time quite smartly. Then back she hopped to the cupboard again, beginning to enjoy herself.

The eight girls in the music-room jumped almost out of their skins when the second knocking came.

"There must be somebody there," said Tessie, quite pale with fright. "I'll go and see."

She went bravely to the door and opened it. There was no one there! Tessie shone her torch into the passage. It was perfectly empty. The girl shut the door and went back to her seat, looking frightened.

"It wasn't any one," she said.

"Stuff and nonsense," said Janet, beginning to recover from her fright. "Doors don't knock by themselves! It must be some one having a joke."

"But, Janet, no one knows we are here," said Isabel.

"Shall we get back to bed – and not fry the sausages?" asked Tessie.

That was too much for Isabel. "What, not fry the sausages when I've been looking forward to them all the evening!" she said, indignantly.

"Shut up, idiot! Do you want to wake the whole school?" said Pat, giving her a nudge that nearly sent her off her chair. "Fry the sausages, Tessie, old girl. I think that knocking must have been the wind!"

So the sausages were fried, and sizzled deliciously in the pan on the top of the oil-stove. Tessie turned them over and over with a fork, trying not to squeal when the hot fat jumped out and burnt her.

Erica had crept out of the cupboard again. She heard the sizzling of the sausages, and the lovely smell made her feel hungry. She wondered what to do next. A noise made her scurry back to the cupboard. What could it be?

Then Erica knew. It was Mam'zelle in her study, having one of her late nights! The French mistress sometimes stayed up very late, reading and studying – and tonight she was still in her study! Erica smiled to herself. She knew what she was going to do now. She wouldn't tell Miss Jenks! She would let hot-tempered Mam'zelle find out – and she herself wouldn't come out into the open at all!

"I'll go and knock at Mam'zelle's door," said Erica to herself. "Then I'll skip back to the dormitory. Mam'zelle will open her door in surprise – and when she finds no one there she'll go and prowl around, if I know anything about her! And it won't be long before she smells those sausages!"

So Erica slipped up the passage to the door of the little room that Mam'zelle used as a study. She knocked smartly on it three times – rap-rap-rap!

"*Tiens!*" came Mam'zelle's voice, in the greatest surprise. "Who is there!"

There was no answer, of course, for Erica had slipped as quietly as a mouse away from the door – not into the cupboard this time, but back into her dormitory. She guessed there would soon be trouble about, and she wasn't going to share in it!

Mam'zelle slid back her chair and went to the door, puzzled. She threw it open, but there was no one there. She stood there for a moment, wondering if she could possibly have been mistaken – and then she heard, from somewhere not very far off, a subdued giggle. And down the passage crept the unmistakable smell of – frying sausages!

Mam'zelle Makes a Discovery

Mam'zelle could not believe her senses. What – frying sausages at a quarter to one at night! It was not possible. She must be dreaming. Mam'zelle gave herself a hard pinch to see if she *was* dreaming or not. No – she was not. She was wide awake! There would be a bruise tomorrow where she had pinched herself.

"But who should be frying sausages at night!" wondered Mam'zelle in amazement. "And where did that laugh come from? Surely not from the dormitory nearby?"

She went to see, shuffling along in her old comfortable slippers. She looked into the dormitory where Tessie and the others slept. She switched on the light. Five of the beds were empty!

Mam'zelle had not been at all good-tempered lately. She had not been sleeping well, and she had been difficult in class. She was tired now, with her hours of studying and correcting, and she felt really angry with the five truants.

"It is too much!" she said to herself, as she switched out the light. "The bad girls! How can they do their lessons well if they are awake to such hours of the night? And they are working for the scholarship exam. too – ah, I shall report them to Miss Theobald!"

Mam'zelle stood in the passage, sniffing. She simply could not imagine where the smell of sausages came from. Then she heard a scuffle and a giggle. It came from the music-room nearby!

Mam'zelle went to the door. She flung it open and glared into the warm little room.

There was a deep silence. Every girl stared in dismay at the large form of the angry French mistress.

"Oh – Mam'zelle – Mam'zelle," stammered Tessie, at last.

"Yes, it is I, Mam'zelle!" said the mistress, her eyes flashing. "And what have you to say for yourselves, acting in this manner at this time of night!"

Tessie couldn't think of a word to say and at last in despair she held out a fried sausage on a fork to Mam'zelle.

"Wouldn't you – wouldn't you have a sausage?" she asked, desperately.

That was too much for Mam'zelle. She didn't see that Tessie was very frightened, she only thought that the girl was being cheeky. And the English "cheek" was something that always made Mam'zelle see red!

She swept the sausage off the fork, and for half a moment Tessie thought that Mam'zelle was going to box her ears. She ducked – and heard Mam'zelle's booming voice above her head.

"So that is the way you would treat your French mistress? Why did I ever come to England to teach such ungrateful girls? You will come straight to Miss Theobald now, all of you!"

There was a moment's intense astonishment and fright. Go to Miss Theobald now – in the middle of the night – when she was alseep in bed! It couldn't be true!

"Please, Mam'zelle," said Janet, who was recovering herself more quickly than the others, "please don't make us do that. Tomorrow morning would do, wouldn't it? We don't want to disturb Miss Theobald now. We're sorry we disturbed you – we thought every one was asleep."

"But one of you knocked on my door!" said Mam'zelle in astonishment. "So – rap-rap-rap." She rapped on the tables as she spoke.

"None of us did that," said Janet, more and more astonished. "Somebody came and knocked on our door too. Whoever could it have been?"

But Mam'zelle was not interested in that. Her rage was gradually dying down as she looked at the white, scared faces of the eight girls. She realized that it was impossible to take them all into Miss Theobald's bedroom. It must wait till tomorrow.

"We will not after all disturb Miss Theobald to-night," she said. "You will all go back to bed – and in the morning you will expect to be called in front of the Head Mistress to explain this dreadful behaviour."

"Could – could we just finish the sausages?" asked Isabel, longingly. But that roused Mam'zelle's anger again. She caught Isabel firmly by the arm and pushed her out of the music-room. "You – a first-form girl – daring to do a thing like this!" she cried. "Go! You should be well slapped, all of you! Go, before I begin to do it!"

The girls were half afraid that Mam'zelle might be as good as her word. They slipped down the passage and into their dormitories, climbing into bed, shivering with fright. What a dreadful ending to a midnight party!

Mam'zelle turned out the light. Then she saw the glow of the oil-stove and turned out that too. "These girls!" she said, pursing up her big lips, "these English girls! How they behave!"

Mam'zelle would never have dared to behave in such a free and easy way at her school in France when she had been a girl. She had worked much harder than any of the girls at St. Clare's. She had played no games, had been for hardly any walks, and had never even seen the inside of a gym until she had come to England. She did not really understand the girls at St. Clare's although she had been there for years, and had taught them well. She was quite determined to have every one of the truants well punished.

She reported them to Miss Theobald before breakfast the next morning. She even took the surprised Head Mistress to the little music-room to show her the remains of the feast. Miss Theobald looked at the ginger-beer bottles, the frying-pan with its congealed fat and few sausages left in it, and the crumbs on the floor.

"I will see the girls at break," said the Head. "This kind of thing cannot be allowed, Mam'zelle – but at some time or other most school-girls attend a midnight feast! Do not take too serious a view of it!"

"In my school-days such a thing was not even thought of!" said Mam'zelle. "Ah, we knew how to work, we French girls!"

'But did you know how to play, Mam'zelle?" asked Miss Theobald, softly. "It is just as important to know how to have good fun – as to do good work, you know!"

Mam'zelle snorted when Miss Theobald left her. She thought that the Head was far too lenient with the girls. She went into the big dining-hall to have breakfast. She glanced round the table where the first and second form sat.

It was easy to pick out the eight girls who had been caught the night before. They were pale and looked tired. Isabel and Susan could not eat any breakfast, partly because they had eaten too much the night before, and partly because they were scared at what might be going to happen to them.

Mam'zelle stopped the eight girls when they filed out of the dining-hall. "You, Janet – and you, Winnie – and you, Susan, and you ... you will all eight go to Miss Theobald at break."

"Yes, Mam'zelle," said the girls, and went to the assembly room for morning prayers and roll-call, feeling rather shaky about the legs!

"Pity we were caught," said Pat to Isabel, in the middle of the hymn. "Now Miss Theobald will think we didn't mean to try to do our best this term. Oh blow, Mam'zelle! Mean old thing! I won't try a bit in French this term now."

The eight girls were bad at their lessons that morning. Erica watched the five in her form, all trying not to yawn, as they did their arithmetic under Miss Jenks's eagle eye.

It was French next, and Tessie put on a sulky face when Mam'zelle entered the room. She felt that she really hated the French mistress that morning. She wasn't going to try a bit!

It wouldn't have mattered if she *had* tried – for poor Tessie was really woolly-headed that day! She had not been able to go to sleep until about five o'clock the night before, and was now so sleepy that her thoughts kept running into one another in a most annoying manner. She was really half asleep.

Mam'zelle chose to think that Tessie was defying her. She scolded the girl roundly, and gave her such a lot of extra prep. to do that poor Tessie was almost in tears.

"But I can't possibly get all that done, Mam'zelle, you know I can't," she protested.

"We shall see!" said Mam'zelle, grimly. And Tessie knew that she would have to do it somehow.

At break the eight girls met together outside the Head Mistress's door. They were all nervous, even Pat who was usually bold. Tessie knocked.

"Come in!" said Miss Theobald's clear voice. They trooped in and shut the door.

Miss Theobald faced them, and looked at each girl seriously. They all felt upset, and Susan began to cry. Then the Head talked to them, and pointed out that it was impossible for good work to be done on half a night's sleep, and that the rules must be kept. She said many other things in her low, calm voice, and the listening girls took it all in.

"Now please understand," said Miss Theobald, "that although you have broken the rule forbidding any girl to leave her dormitory at night, your escapade is not in the same rank as, for instance, meanness, lying, or disloyalty. Those are serious things – what you have done might be serious if you were allowed to do it often – but I regard it more as silly mischief. But even silly mischief has to be punished – and so you will not be allowed to go down into the town for two weeks. That means no walks together, no shopping, and no visits to the tea-shop or to the cinema."

There was a silence. This was a horrid punishment. The girls really loved their privilege of going down to the town in twos, spending their pocket-money, and going to the tea-shop for tea. Two weeks seemed a very, very long time.

But nobody dared to protest. They all knew that Miss Theobald was absolutely just. "You see," the Head went on, "if you behave like small children instead of senior girls, I shall have to treat you as small children, and take away your senior privileges. Now you may go. Tessie, see that the mess in the music-room is cleared up before dinner-time, please."

"Yes, Miss Theobald," said Tessie, meekly, and all eight girls filed out of the room.

"Well, I'm glad that's over," said Pat, when they were out of ear-shot of the drawing-room. "And there's another thing I'm glad about too – that Miss Theobald made that distinction between mischief and mean things. I wouldn't like her to think we'd do anything mean or rotten. A joke's a joke – ours went too far, that's all."

"Yes," said Isabel, thoughtfully. "But there's one very mean thing about this, Pat – and that is – the knocking on Mam'zelle's door, that told her something was up! That's the meanest thing I ever heard of! We'll have to find out who did it – and punish them!"

A Bad Time for Erica

Erica was pleased when she heard of the punishment meted out to the eight girls. She did not dare to say much because she was so afraid that she might be found out. She knew quite well that the girls must wonder who had made the knocking on the doors.

The girls meant to find out who the tale-teller was. They met that evening, and discussed the matter.

"She shan't get away with it," declared Tessie, fiercely. "Golly, wasn't I astonished when Mam'zelle let out that she had been disturbed by some one knocking at her door! It must have been the same horrible person who came knocking at ours to give us a fright and spoil the party. I'm sorry I asked you all now. It was my fault."

"It was jolly decent of you to think of giving us a treat," said Pat. "Don't apologize for that! Nobody would have known a thing about it if it hadn't been for that wretched spoil-sport."

"Pat," said Tessie, suddenly, "you don't think it would have been that silly cousin of yours, do you? You know how she bleats everything all over the place. You didn't tell her anything, did you?"

Pat flushed. "Not a word," she said, "and look here, Tessie, though you've got a pretty poor opinion of

Alison – and so have I – she's not the sort to sneak. Honestly she isn't. She can't keep her tongue still – but she wouldn't do a thing like giving us away to Mam'zelle."

"All right," said Tessie. "Well – I simply don't know who it was – and I don't see how we're to find out! Every one in our dormitory seemed to be asleep when we got back."

"And so did every one in ours," said Pat. "It's a puzzle. But I'm going to find out who it was, Tessie. I feel so angry when I think about it. I shan't rest till I know who it was."

They all felt like that, but it was impossible to find out – or so it seemed! Every one denied even having known that the party was to take place – though most of the girls said that they guessed something was up.

Alison denied absolutely that she knew anything. "And if I had, I wouldn't have split for worlds," she said, an angry flush on her cheek. "You might know that. You don't seem to have much opinion of me lately, you two – but you might at least know that."

"We do know that," Pat hastened to say. "But it *is* funny, Alison, that although nobody seems to know anything about the party, somebody knew enough to scare us and to bring Mam'zelle out on the war-path!"

It was quite by accident that the truth came out. Gladys, the little scullery-maid, came upstairs to find the frying-pan she had lent to Tessie. It had not been brought back to her, and she was afraid that the cook might miss it.

She couldn't find Tessie, but she met Pat on the stairs. "Oh, Miss Patricia," she said, "could you get me back the frying-pan I lent Miss Tessie for the party? I can't find her. I could have asked Miss Erica, but she disappeared before I could speak to her."

"Miss Erica wouldn't have known anything about it," said Pat. "She didn't go to the party."

"Oh, but Miss Patricia, she *did* know about it," said the small scullery-maid. "I met her when I was bringing it upstairs – and she pulled aside my apron and saw the frying-pan, and she said, in that haughty way of hers – "Oho, for Miss Tessie's party!""

Pat was astonished. It might have been a guess on Erica's part, of course – but anyway, she had seen the frying-pan – and, if she knew anything about sneaky Erica, she would certainly have kept watch, and have put two and two together – and found out everything without difficulty!

"I said to Miss Erica, I said 'Well, miss, if you knew what the frying-pan was for, why did you ask me?' " said Gladys, quite enjoying this talk with Pat. 'Oh dear, miss – I heard you'd got into trouble over the party, and I'm so sorry."

"I'll get you the frying-pan," said Pat, and she went to the music-room, where the pan sat solemnly on top of the piano, cleaned by one of the second-formers, but otherwise forgotten.

Gladys took it and scuttled downstairs thankfully. She was just as much in awe of the cook as the girls were in awe of Miss Theobald!

Pat went to find Isabel. She told her what Gladys had said. "It was Erica all right," said Pat, fiercely. "I'm not a bit surprised either, are you? Every one says she's a sneak. That's almost one of the worst things you can be. Whatever will Tessie say?"

Tessie said a lot. She was angry and indignant. To think that a girl who had shared her chocolates and her birthday cake could have played such a mean trick!

"We'll jolly well tackle her about it," said Tessie. "After tea today. You come into the common room,

48

Pat — and we'll have it out with her. I'll tell the others."

"Yes, but every one else will be there," said Pat, uneasily. "Is it quite fair to let every one hear?"

"Why not?" said Tessie, angrily. "A sneak deserves to be denounced in public. Anyway, we can't go anywhere else."

So after tea that day Erica was called by Pat. She was sitting in a corner, writing a letter home.

"Erica, come over here. We want to speak to you," said Pat, in a cold voice. Erica looked up. She went pale. Could the girls have discovered her mean trick?

"I'm busy," she said, sulkily. "I've got to finish this letter."

She went on writing. Pat lost her temper and snatched away the letter. "You jolly well come!" she said, fiercely. "Do you want me and Isabel to lug you over?"

Erica saw that there was nothing for it but to go to the corner of the common room where the six other girls were waiting for her.

She went, looking pale and sulky. She was determined to deny everything.

"Erica, we know that it was you who knocked on the music-room door the other night," said Pat. "And it was you too who gave the game away to Mam'zelle and got us punished. You're a mean pig, a horrid sneak, and you're jolly well going to be punished!"

"I don't know what you are talking about," said Erica, in a trembling voice, not daring to meet eight pairs of accusing eyes.

"Yes, you do. It's no good pretending," said Tessie. "Pat has found out everything. Every single thing. We know that you met Gladys on the stairs when she was bringing up something for us."

"I don't know anything about the frying-pan," said Erica.

49

Pat pounced at once. "How do you know that it was a frying-pan that Gladys was bringing us? There you are, you see – you do know. You've convicted yourself out of your own mouth!"

The other girls in the common room, curious to hear what was going on, came round, peeping. Alison came too, her big blue eyes almost popping out of her head.

"Oh, was it Erica who gave you away?" she said. "Well, I might have guessed! She was always bothering me to find out from you and Isabel, Pat, what the secret was."

"Well, it's a good thing for you, Alison, that for once you had the common sense not to give anything away," said Pat, grimly. "Now, Erica – you're a horrible sneak – but at least you might have the decency to own up!"

"I don't know anything about it," said Erica, stubbornly. "It's no good your going on at me like this – I just simply don't know anything about it."

"Go on, Erica, own up!" cried half a dozen voices from members of the second form, who were now all crowding round in the greatest curiosity.

But Erica wouldn't. She hadn't the sense to see that if she owned up frankly and could even bring herself to say she was sorry, the other girls would at least respect her for confessing.

As it was, she made them all intensely angry. "Very well," said Pat. "Don't own up. But you'll have two punishments instead of one, that's all. You'll be punished for sneaking – and you'll be punished for not owning up too!"

"Yes," said Tessie. "And the punishment for sneaking is that you jolly well won't go down into the town for two weeks, like us. See?"

"I shall," said Erica.

"Well, you won't," said Tessie. "I'm head of the

50

second form, and I forbid *any* one to go with you – and you know you are not allowed to go alone. So there!"

Erica was beaten and she knew it. No girl dared to go to the town alone, for that was strictly forbidden. She flushed and said nothing.

"And the punishment for not owning up decently we leave to the first and second forms," said Pat, her eyes flashing round. "I am sure that not one of us, Erica, wants to speak to you, or have anything more to do with you than we can help! That's always the punishment for your sort of behaviour!"

"*I* shan't speak to her," muttered several girls around. Every one felt disgusted with the miserable Erica. She would have a bad time! It is hard to see glances of contempt and dislike wherever you look, and to have nobody saying a jolly word.

Erica went off to her corner, but her hand trembled as she tried to finish her letter. She was ashamed – but she was angry too – and with Pat most of all!

"So she found out, did she, and told all the others!" thought Erica. "All right, Pat – I'll pay you out for that – and your silly twin too!"

Margery Gets a Chance

The first form did not really see very much of Erica, because she did not have lessons with them. But if ever they met her in a passage or in the art room or gym, they looked the other way. In the common room at night Erica had a miserable time. Not one of the second-form girls would have anything to do with her.

Loud remarks about sneaks and cowards were made in her hearing. The only person who ever threw her a word at all was the bad-tempered Margery Fenworthy. Erica did not like Margery, any more than the other girls did, but she was so grateful to be spoken to, even by the surly first-former, that she almost began to like the girl.

"I'm surprised you speak to Erica, Margery," said Pat when she had heard Margery ask to borrow Erica's paints.

"Mind your own business," said Margery, in her usual rude way. "You're none of you friendly to me, and I know what it is to have people being so beastly to you."

"But Margery, it's your own fault," said Pat, in surprise. "You're so rude and sullen. You never smile and joke."

"Well, people never smile and joke with *me*," said Margery. "You don't give me a chance."

"Oh, Margery, what a fib!" cried Pat. "It's you who never give *us* a chance to be decent to you. You scowl and glower and frown all the time."

"If you're going to pick me to pieces you can save yourself the trouble," said Margery, fiercely. "I don't care tuppence for any of you. And if I want to speak to that wretched Erica, I shall. Who cares for a pack of silly girls, and a crowd of stuck-up teachers? I don't!"

Pat was astonished. What a strange girl Margery was! Did she really want a chance of being friends with the others? Was she terribly shy – what was behind that funny manner of hers?

Pat talked about it with her twin. "Margery is always making enemies," she said, "I spoke to her today about it – and she accused us of never giving her a chance. Do you think we ought to do something about it?"

"Ask Lucy," said Isabel, seeing Lucy coming up to show them a picture she had just finished. "Oh, Lucy – what a marvellous drawing! It's Mam'zelle to the life!"

Lucy had a clever pencil with portraits. She could, with a few strokes of her pencil, draw any girl or teacher so that every one knew at once who it was. The drawing she held out was excellent.

"It's exactly how Mam'zelle looks when she says, 'Ah, Dorrrrr-is, you are insupportable!'" said Pat. "Lucy, listen, we've been talking about Margery."

"I'll draw her," said Lucy. She sat down and sketched Margery's sullen good-looking face – and then, in a few strokes she sketched another Margery – a smiling one, most delightful to see.

"Before taking a course of St. Clare's – and after!" laughed Lucy.

"Golly – that's clever," said Isabel. "It's a pity Margery can't always look like that second drawing. Listen now, Lucy. She told Pat this morning that we've never given her a chance to be friendly."

"All wrong," said Lucy, beginning to draw again. "*She* has never given *us* a chance!"

"Exactly what I said," said Pat, eagerly. "Oh, Lucy, is that Erica? Goodness, what a poor creature she looks!"

"And is," said Lucy. "I'll be glad when we can speak to her again, in a way. I hate to be beastly to anyone even if they deserve it. It makes me feel horrible myself."

"Lucy, do you think we'd better give Margery a chance, even though she's so jolly difficult?" asked Pat. "You know – Isabel and I were simply awful last term – and every one was decent to us. It seems only fair for us to be decent to somebody else who's new, and who seems awful too."

"I'm all for it," said Lucy, shaking back her dark curls from her friendly, pretty face. "My father says 'Always give the under-dog a chance' – and for some reason or other poor Margery seems to think she's an under-dog – every one's hand against her – that sort of thing. Goodness knows why she's got that idea, but she has. All right – I'll go out of my way to be friendly, if you will."

"We'll tell the others, as well," said Pat. So the first-formers were told about the idea, and although most of them thought it was stupid, because they really did dislike Margery, they all agreed to back up Lucy and the twins. Even Alison said she would – and she had suffered very much from Margery's rudeness. Margery thought Alison a silly little feather-head, and had said so, many times.

So, what with avoiding Erica, and trying to be nice to Margery, things were quite exciting. The first time that Margery showed any signs of being pleased was when the first form were in the gym. Margery was ex-cellent at climbing, jumping, and any kind of exercise. When she did an extra good jump in the gym, the girls clapped.

Margery glanced round, surprised. She gave a half-smile, and stepped to her place. The mistress spoke a few words of praise too. Margery tried not too look too pleased, but she couldn't help going red with pleasure.

Afterwards Pat spoke to her. "Margery, you're jolly good at gym," she said. "I wish I could climb and jump like you."

"I like anything like that," said Margery, in a civil tone. "As for games, I simply adore them. I only wish we could play three times as much as we do! I wish we went riding more here too. I used to love that at my old school."

"What school did you go to before you came here?" asked Isabel, pleased to see that Margery could really talk quite normally!

But for some reason or other Margery would not say any more. She turned away and her old scowling look came over her face. The twins were disappointed.

All the same, Margery felt that every one was giving her a chance, and she did respond in many ways. She didn't give so many rude answers, and she did occasionally offer to help any one in difficulties. She even offered to give silly little Alison some practise at catching the ball in lacrosse, because she saw that the twins were really ashamed of their cousin's stupidity at games.

But Alison refused. "Why does every one keep badgering me to practise catching?" she grumbled. "I hate lacrosse. I hate all games. I hate having to run across a dirty field and get hot and out of breath. We all look awful when we've finished playing!"

"Alison! Is there ever a time when you don't think about how you look?" cried Janet. "You're as vain as a peacock. I hope you get a whole lot of spots tomorrow!"

"Don't be mean!" said Alison, the easy tears coming into her eyes.

"Well, for goodness' sake act more like a senior girl and not like a baby," grumbled Janet. "Your cousins were bad enough when they came last term – but at least they didn't turn on the water-tap like you do, at any minute of the day!"

"I should think not!" said Pat, hotly, ready to attack Janet, who was in one of her sharp-tongued moods.

But Janet gave her a friendly punch. She never wanted to quarrel with the twins, whom she sincerely liked.

Although Margery seemed to be much more friendly with the girls, she was no better with the mistresses, to whom she was really rude. She did not try at all with her lessons – and the curious thing was that all the mistresses seemed to have endless patience with the sulky girl.

"Golly! If any of us were half as rude to Miss Roberts as Margery is, we'd soon hear about it," said Pat, half a dozen times a week. "I can't understand it. Did you see the work that Margery handed in to Miss Lewis too? She only did half a page, and her writing was awful."

"Well, what about her arithmetic!" said Hilary. "Honestly, I don't think she got a single sum right this morning – and Miss Roberts never said a word."

"She won't say how old she is," said Pat. "I believe Margery's sixteen! And most of us in the first form are fourteen or just fifteen."

"Oh well – never mind. She can't help being stupid, I suppose," said Lucy. "Anyway, she's jolly good at games – and when we play that match against the Oakdene girls next week, I bet we'll be glad of Margery. She's been put into the match-team, you know."

"Has she?" said Pat. "Golly! I wish I'd been put in it too. I haven't seen the list."

"Well, you're not in it," said Janet. "I've looked. No first-former except Margery is in it – and only two second-formers! The rest are all third-formers. It's an honour for Margery to be chosen – but honestly, she's frightfully good at games, and most awfully quick and strong."

"Well, if she's sixteen, as you say, she *ought* to be quick and strong," said Alison, cattily.

56

"Shut up, Alison," said Pat. "We don't *know* that she's sixteen. Now don't you go round bleating about *that*!"

"I *don't* bleat," began Alison, in her pathetic voice, making her blue eyes very wide and hurt. But half a dozen exasperated girls yelled at her and threw cushions – so Alison thought it better to say no more. No one could bear Alison when she went "all goofy" as Janet described it.

When the two weeks were nearly up, and the eight girls were looking forward to being allowed to go down into the town again, the Big Row had happened. It all centred around Margery, who in ten minutes, destroyed the new friendliness that had begun to grow up around her.

It happened in history class, and blew up all in a minute. The girls were horrified – and ever afterwards it was spoken of as the Big Row.

The Big Row

Miss Lewis was taking the history lesson, and the class were learning about the discovery of America, and its conquest. As usual the class was giving the history teacher close attention, for if there was one thing that Miss Lewis would not put up with, it was inattention.

Even Margery usually attended to Miss Lewis more than to the other teachers – partly because she was interested in history, and partly because she was a little afraid of Miss Lewis and her sharp eyes.

But this morning something seemed to have happened to Margery. The girls had noticed it from the time she had sat down to breakfast. There had been a letter by her plate which Margery had not opened until she had been by herself. From that time onwards Margery had gone back to her most sullen and don't-care self – though nobody imagined that it was anything to do with the letter, of course.

She had been careless and inattentive in Miss Roberts's arithmetic class, and Miss Roberts had been, as usually, patient with her. In the French class, after a sharp look at her, Mam'zelle had taken no notice of Margery, but had let her sit and sulk to herself.

She had cheered up a little in the history class, but had not taken any party in the discussion that Miss Lewis sometimes allowed at the beginning of the lesson.

Then Hilary had come out with a good idea. "Miss Lewis! There's a play on in the next town, at the Royal Theatre – and it's called 'Drake'. Would it be about the same period of history that we're doing?"

"Oh, yes," said Miss Lewis. "It's a fine play. Just the right period."

"Oh, Miss Lewis – do you think you could possibly take us to see it!" cried Hilary, who adored plays of any kind.

"Oh, yes, Miss Lewis!" cried the rest of the form, eagerly. "An outing to the next town would be marvellous."

"Hush," said Miss Lewis, rapping on her desk. "Do remember there are other classes going on. When is the play being performed, Hilary?"

Hilary had a notice of it in her desk. She rummaged about and found it. "There's a special performance on Saturday afternoon, this week," she said. "Oh Miss Lewis – do, do take us! I'd love to see it."

"That's my week-end off," said Miss Lewis, regretfully. "I'd arranged to go for a walking-tour with Miss Walker. We've got it all planned."

Each mistress had a week-end off during the term, and they looked forward to this very much. The class knew how precious the week-ends were to the staff, and they stared in disappointment at Miss Lewis. What a pity! Just the Saturday the play was on. It would have been such fun to go and see it.

"Oh, blow!" said Pat. "Wouldn't that just be the way! Never mind, Miss Lewis – it can't be helped."

"Well – I don't know," said Miss Lewis, slowly. "Perhaps it *can* be helped! You've been good workers this term, and maybe I could give up the Saturday to take you – and go home on the Sunday morning, for one day instead of two. Miss Walker can find some one else to go walking with, I daresay."

"Oh, I say – we wouldn't let you do that," said Janet, at once. "We're not quite such selfish pigs, Miss Lewis."

Miss Lewis laughed. She liked the outspoken first-formers. "I'll arrange it," she said. "I'll speak to Miss Theobald – and the whole class can go with me in the school bus. We'll book seats at the Royal Theatre, and go and have a lovely time seeing the play – and we'll have a marvellous tea afterwards."

There were sighs and squeals of delight. Shining eyes looked at Miss Lewis, and every one beamed with joy. What an unexpected treat! Even Margery Fenworthy looked pleased.

"Miss Lewis, you're a sport!" said Janet. "You really are! Thanks most awfully. Are you really sure you don't mind taking us on your precious week-end?"

"Oh, I mind awfully," said Miss Lewis, with a twinkle in her eye. "Do you suppose it's any pleasure to me to take charge of twenty noisy first-formers with no manners at all?"

Every one laughed. Miss Lewis might be sharp at

times – but she really was a good sort!

"Now mind –" said Miss Lewis, warningly. "You will all work well to show me that you really do appreciate the treat! No slacking this term!"

"Of course not!" said the girls, quite determined to work better for Miss Lewis than they had ever done before.

Ten minutes later came the Big Row. Each girl had her history book open, and was following the map there that Miss Lewis was explaining – all except Margery. She had her book open it was true – but into the open pages she had slipped the letter she had received that morning, and she was re-reading it, a scowl on her face.

Miss Lewis spoke to Margery and got no answer. The girl didn't hear the question at all. She was so engrossed in her own thoughts. Miss Lewis spoke again, sharply.

"Margery! You are not paying the least attention! What is that you have in your book?"

"Nothing," said Margery, with a jump. She tried to slip the letter out of the pages. Miss Lewis looked angry.

"Bring me that letter," she said.

"It's mine," said Margery, with her sullenest look. "I know that," said Miss Lewis, irritably. "You can give it to me till the end of the morning. Then there will not be any temptation for you to read it in another lesson. You certainly will not do a thing like that in *my* lesson again. Bring me the letter."

"What! For you to read!" flared up Margery in a rage. "Nobody's going to read my private letters!"

"Margery! You forget yourself," said Miss Lewis, coldly. "Do you suppose I should read the letter? You know better than that. But I shall certainly confiscate it for the rest of the day now. You will bring me the letter, and you will come to me for it this evening, and apologize for your behaviour."

"I shan't do anything of the sort," said Margery, rudely. All the girls stared in horror.

"Shut up, Margery," said Pat, who was sitting next to her. "Don't you dare to speak like that!"

"*You* shut up!" said Margery, turning a look of rage on Pat. "I won't be interfered with by anybody – no, not even by Miss Theobald herself! As for Miss Lewis, with her sharp eyes and her sharp nose sticking into my private business, she won't get anything out of *me*!"

"Margery!" cried half a dozen voices in the utmost horror. Nobody could believe their ears. Margery was flushed a bright red, and her eyes flashed angrily. She was in her worst temper, and she didn't care in the least what she said.

Miss Lewis was very angry. She was white, and her nose looked suddenly rather thin, as it always did when she was cross. But this morning she was more than cross. She stood up.

"Leave the room, Margery," she said, in a cold quiet voice. "I shall have to consider whether or not I can have you in my history classes again."

"I'll leave the room all right," said Margery. "I'd leave the whole school, if I could! I didn't want to come. I knew what would happen! I hate the lot of you!"

The angry girl walked out, her head held high. But once outside she leaned her head against the wall and cried bitterly. She was shocked and upset.

Miss Theobald happened to come along just as Margery was wiping her eyes, and wondering where to go. She looked at Margery in silence.

"Come with me, my dear," she said. "Something has happened, hasn't it? You must tell me about it."

"It's no good," said Margery. "I'll be sent away from here. And I don't care. I don't care a bit."

"Yes, you do care," said Miss Theobald. "You care a lot. Margery, come with me. Come along, please. We can't stand out here like this. The girls will be pouring out of the classrooms in a little while."

Margery took a look at Miss Theobald's calm serious face. The Head looked at Margery with a wise and compassionate glance in her deep eyes. The angry girl gave a sob, and then went with the Head Mistress.

Inside the classroom there was a babel of furious voices.

"The beast! How could she behave like that!"

"Just after Miss Lewis had said she'd give up her Saturday too!"

"It's a waste of time to be nice to a creature like that! I'll never speak to her again!"

"She deserves to be expelled! I shouldn't be surprised if she is!"

"Miss Lewis! We all apologize to you for Margery! We do really."

"Girls, girls, be quiet, please," said Miss Lewis, putting on her glasses and looking round the room. "There is no need to make a noise like this. We have only five minutes of this lesson left. Turn to page fifty-six, please. I don't want to hear another word about Margery."

So no more was said in class – but plenty was said outside! How they raged against her! The second form heard about it too, and they were amazed and aghast that any one should dare to behave like that to Miss Lewis.

"I wish I'd been there," said Tessie, who always enjoyed a row, so long as she wasn't the centre of it. "Golly! Miss Lewis must have been furious!"

"Where's Margery now?" asked Pat.

Nobody knew. She didn't appear again at all that morning or afternoon – but after tea she came into the common room, rather white, and looking defiant, for she guessed how the girls felt about her.

"Here comes the meanie!" said Janet. "I hope you're ashamed of yourself, Margery!"

But Margery refused to say a single word. She sat in a corner, reading – or pretending to read – and would not answer anything said to her. The girls gave her a bad time. Even Erica was forgotten. In fact Erica seemed quite harmless, somehow, after the dreadful way Margery had behaved!

"I wonder if Margery will be allowed to come to the history lesson tomorrow," said Janet. "I bet Miss Lewis won't let her!"

But there was a surprise in store for the class when Miss Lewis came to take history next day. Margery was there too!

"Good morning, girls," said Miss Lewis, as she came into the room. "Margery, will you go and speak to Mam'zelle for a minute? She is in her study and wants a word with you. Come back when she has finished."

Margery went out, looking surprised. Miss Lewis turned to the girls. "I just want to say that Margery has apologized for her bad behaviour," said Miss Lewis. "She had a talk with Miss Theobald who found her, outside the classroom, and she came to me yesterday evening to apologize. I have accepted her apology and am taking her back into my class. I hardly think such a thing will happen again, and I would like you all to forget it as soon as possible, please."

"But, Miss Lewis – isn't she going to be punished?" asked Janet, indignantly.

"Perhaps she has been," said Miss Lewis, putting on her glasses. "I think we can safely leave things to be decided by the Head Mistress, don't you? Now, not a word more about the subject, please. Turn to page fifty-six."

The class were turning to page fifty-six when Margery came back. Mam'zelle had wanted her about a very small thing, and the girl could not help feeling that she had been sent out for a few minutes so that Miss Lewis could say something about her. She walked to her desk, red in the face, and found her place. She paid great attention to the lesson, and Miss Lewis hadn't the slightest reason to find fault with her that morning.

But at break the girls had a great deal to say about Margery again! "Forget it as soon as possible!" snorted Janet. "How could Miss Lewis say a thing like that? Golly, I think Margery ought to have been expelled from the school! After we'd tried to be so decent to her too. You just simply CAN'T help a girl like that."

So once more Margery was sent back to her lonely, friendless state. No one spoke to her if they could help it, and nobody even looked at her.

"It's a pity she's playing in the match," said Pat. "Well – *I* shan't clap if she shoots a goal!"

The days went quickly by. The first form were taken to the play, and enjoyed every minute of it. They had a wonderful tea afterwards, for Miss Lewis really did do things well!

"Buns and jam! Fruit cake! Meringues! Chocolate éclairs!" said Janet, describing it all to the envious second-formers when they got back. "Golly, it *was* a spread! I don't know which I enjoyed most – the play or the tea. They were both marvellous."

"Did Margery go too?" asked Tessie, curiously. Every one, of course, had heard of the Big Row. Even the top-formers knew about it.

"Yes – she went," said Pat. "Though if it had been me I wouldn't have had the cheek to have gone. She didn't say a word the whole time – but she thanked Miss Lewis for taking her. Personally I think it was jolly sporting of Miss Lewis even to *think* of having her!"

"So do I," said Tessie. "I heard Belinda say yesterday that if Margery wasn't so awfully good at lacrosse, she would strike her out of the match. She's very fond of Miss Lewis, you know, and she was furious when she heard how Margery had cheeked her."

"Well, it's about the only good thing you can say of Margery – that she's good at games," said Tessie. "But my word, she's fierce, isn't she! I hope Belinda will give her a word of warning before the match. If she tackles the Oakdene team too savagely she'll be sent off the field. And then we shall be one man short."

Belinda did warn Margery. The match was to

65

be played on the home-field, and the whole school was to watch, if it was fine. Oakdene and St. Clare's were well-matched. There wasn't much to choose between them. So far the score was eleven matches won by each, so this match would be rather exciting.

"Margery, don't be hauled up on a foul, please," said Belinda to the girl as she was changing into her gym things before the match. "You lose your head sometimes and forget you're so strong. Play fairly, and you'll be jolly useful. Lose your temper and you'll probably be sent off the field!"

Margery scowled and said nothing. She bent over to put on her shoes. Pat and Janet came into the changing room to look for Isabel and Alison.

"Oh, there you are!" said Pat, seeing the other two. It was dark in the changing-room and she did not see Margery, bending down over her shoes. "Now don't forget, everybody, if that miserable Margery shoots a goal, we don't clap and we don't cheer. See?"

"Right, Pat," said the others. "She doesn't deserve even a whisper – and she won't get it!"

"You horrid beast, Pat!" said Margery, suddenly, standing up in anger. "So that's what you've planned to do, have you! Just like you!"

The four girls stared in dismay. None of them had known that Margery was there.

"I don't want your claps or your cheers," said Margery, stalking out. "One day, Pat, I'll get even with you! You see if I don't!"

The bell rang for the players to take their places. Margery went on to the field, a tall and scowling figure.

"I'm sorry for the girls she's got to play against!" said Belinda to Rita. "My word, she's an extraordinary girl!"

66

The whistle went for the game to begin. It was a fine afternoon, rather cold, but with no wind. The watching girls had on their warm coats and felt hats. They put their hands in their pockets as they sat on the forms, and prepared to shout and cheer and clap when the right times came.

It was always fun to watch a match. It was lovely to be able to yell as loudly as they liked, and to dance about and cheer if anything really exciting happened. The school was always glad when the match was an at-home one, then they could see every goal, and watch all that happened, instead of having to wait until the team came back from an away match.

The game was a bit slow at first. The players hadn't warmed up to it, and every one was playing rather cautiously. No one above the third from was playing in either school. The Oakdene girls did not look a very big lot, but they were wiry and ran fast. They soon got into the game, and the running, tackling and catching began to get very swift and exciting.

"Go it, Susan! Go it, Tessie!" yelled the second-formers, anxious to cheer on their members. Except for the first-former, Margery, all the rest but Tessie and Susan were third-form girls, Margery was the tallest, strongest girl of the home team, even bigger than the third-formers.

"Well run, Mary! Shoot, shoot!" yelled the school, seeing a swift third-former catch the ball from Tessie and tear down the field to the goal. But the Oakdene girl marking her was swift too. She tried to knock the ball from Mary's lacrosse net. Mary swung her net in front of her. The Oakdene girl tried to out-run her but couldn't. She yelled to another girl.

"Tackle her, tackle her!"

Like a hare another Oakdene girl shot out from her

place and ran straight at Mary. The two met with a clash. Mary went spinning, and the ball rolled from her net. The Oakdene girl picked it up neatly and tore back in the opposite direction.

"On her, Margery!" yelled Belinda, from the onlookers. "Go on, go on – run. You can do it?"

Margery Fenworthy shot up like a bullet from a gun! She could run faster than anyone on the field. She raced across to the running girl and did a neat turn round her to get to her lacrosse net. She slashed upwards viciously with her own net – the ball jerked out and Margery caught it deftly. The Oakdene girl slashed back at Margery's net to get the ball, but Margery had already thrown it hard across the field to where Tessie was waiting for it. Down to the goal sped Tessie. She shot – but alas, the ball rolled wide, and the whistle blew.

"My word, that girl Margery plays well," said Rita. Nobody, however, had cheered Margery on as she had tackled the girl and got the ball. But how they yelled to Tessie when she had tried to shoot!

The match went on its exciting way. The school yelled itself hoarse as the battle went first this way and then that way. They teams were beautifully matched, there was no doubt about that.

Margery stood out among all the players. She always played well – but today she seemed inspired. Pat knew why, and felt a little uncomfortable.

"She always plays extra well when she's angry," said Pat to her twin. "Have you noticed that? She seems to make the game into a fight and goes all out for it. Perhaps it helps her to work off her bad temper."

Margery soon got the ball again by a swift piece of running. She dodged a girl running at her, and looked for some one to pass to. Susan was ready. Margery

Margery shot up the field like a bullet

threw the ball to her. Susan caught it, was tackled, and threw the ball back to Margery. There was a clear space to goal. Should she run nearer and shoot, risking being tackled – or should she try one of her long hard shots?

A girl shot out to tackle her. Margery raised her net, and shot the ball hard and strong down the field. It went like a bullet! The tackling girl tried to stop it but failed. The goal-keeper saw it coming and put out her net – but the shot was so hard that she couldn't stop it! The ball was in the goal!

"Goal!" yelled the school. And then there was a silence. There was no clapping. No cheering. No shouts of "Well done, Margery!" It was strange, because after a goal every one usually yelled their loudest. The watching mistresses looked at one another with pursed lips and raised eyebrows. No girl had ever been so unpopular before as not to be cheered in a match!

Half-time came. Pat ran out with a plate of lemon quarters for the thirsty players. How good they tasted! So sour and clean.

"You've got a good player in your team this term," said the captain of the other side, to Pat, as she took her piece of lemon. "But golly, isn't she big? I should have thought she was a top-former."

"Well, she's not," said Pat. "She's in the first form!"

"Gracious!" said the girl, staring at Margery in surprise. Margery was not speaking to any of her team, and no one was speaking to her. "She doesn't seem very popular," said the Oakdene girl. "What's up?"

"Oh, nothing," said Pat, who was not going to talk about Margery's affairs to any one else. "Have another piece of lemon?"

70

"Thanks," said the girl. "My word, this is a good match. Anybody's game, really. You're one goal up – but I bet we get even this half!"

The whistle blew. Pat scurried off the field. The players took their places, at opposite ends to the ones they had had before. The game began again.

It was fast and furious. Every one was now well-warmed-up and enjoying the game. The Oakdene captain scored an unexpected goal, which Bertha, in goal, should have been able to stop and didn't. The whole school groaned. Poor Bertha went as red as fire.

"One all! Play up, St. Clare's!" yelled every one.

If Margery had played well the first half, she played even better in the second half. She ran like the wind, she tackled fearlessly, she caught accurately and threw well. But she unfortunately lost her temper with an Oakdene girl who neatly dodged her with the ball, and brought down her net with such force on the girl's hand to make her drop the ball that the Oakdene girl squealed in pain. The referee blew her whistle and called Margery to her.

"Gosh! Is she going to send her off the field for a foul?" groaned Belinda, who badly wanted her team to win. "She deserves it, I know – she's such a savage when she gets excited – but we can't afford to lose her just now!"

But Margery fortunately was not sent off. She was severely reprimanded, and walked back to her place with the usual sullen look on her face. She was much more careful after that, for she hadn't the slightest wish to be sent off in the middle of such an exciting match.

She got the ball again within the next few minutes, and ran for goal. She passed to Mary, who passed back.

Margery shot – and the ball rolled straight into the corner of the goal, though the goal-keeper frantically tried to stop it.

"Goal!" yelled the whole school. But again there was that curious silence afterwards. No cheering, no clapping. Margery noticed it at once, and her eyes flashed with anger. The beasts! She was playing her best for the school – and yet they wouldn't even give her a cheer! All because of that hateful Pat O'Sullivan!

The girl felt a fury of anger rising up in her. Somehow it gave her even more swiftness and strength than before. She was a miracle of swiftness as she darted about the field, tackling and dodging, getting the ball when it seemed almost impossible.

"If only Oakdene don't shoot again!" cried Pat, in the greatest excitement. "Oh, golly – they're going to. Save it, Bertha, save it!"

But poor Bertha couldn't possibly save the goal that time, though she threw herself flat down on her front to do so. The ball trickled by and came to rest in the goal. Two goals all – and five minutes to play!

And in that five minutes Margery managed to shoot two of the finest goals that any of the school had ever seen. The first one was one of her long shots, straight and true, from half-way down the field. The second was extraordinary. She could not shoot because two girls tackled her just near the goal, and Margery rolled over and over on the ground. The Oakdene girls tried to get the ball from her net but somehow or other Margery managed to hold it safely there – and suddenly, from her position flat on the ground, her nose almost in the mud, Margery jerked her lacrosse net! The ball flew out – and landed in the goal right through the surprised goal-keeper's legs!

At first nobody knew it was a goal – and then the

umpire shouted "Goal! Four goals to St. Clare's, two goals to Oakdene. One more minute to play!"

But before the ball was in play again, time was up. The whistle blew and the players trooped off the field. What a match it had been!

Erica Gets Her Own Back

Usually, after a match, the girls who had shot the winning goals were surrounded, patted and cheered. If any one deserved to be cheered that afternoon it was certainly Margery, for she had done the hardest work, and had stood out as the finest player in the team.

Belinda muttered "Well done!" as Margery came by.

But nobody else said a word. No one went to Margery to clap her on the shoulder. No one shouted "Well played, old girl!" No one, in fact, took any notice of her at all.

The Oakdene girls couldn't help noticing this curious behaviour, and were surprised. They stared hard at Margery, who stared back, her head held high.

"I'm glad we won the match – but I wish it hadn't been Margery who did it all," said Pat. "I feel a bit uncomfortable now about not cheering her a bit. Do you think we ought to go and say a word to her, Janet?"

"Of course we ought!" said Janet, "but you know jolly well what would happen if we did! She'd bite our heads off – and I don't wonder! No – we've started this uncomfortable game of sending some one to Coventry – and we've got to stick to it."

Brave as Margery was, she could not face the school-tea with the teams. Usually after a match the two opposing teams had a special tea to themselves, apart from the rest of the school, though in the same dining-hall of course. At the long team-table they chattered and laughed and discussed the match with one another. The home team acted as hostesses to the visiting team, and it was all great fun.

"It's so lovely when you're tired and happy to sit down to buns and butter and fruit cake and chocolate biscuits and big cups of tea!" sighed Tessie. "And to talk as much as you like about the match. Come on, Susan. I'm ready."

Every one noticed that Margery was not at the table. No one liked to say anything about it. The visiting team were quite aware that there was something queer in the air and did not like to discuss it. The St. Clare team wondered where Margery was, and looked to see if she was at the table where the first-formers were sitting eating their own tea.

But she wasn't. She had gone to the changing-room and changed. Then she had slipped into the deserted class-room and gone to her desk. She was tired, angry and miserable. She wanted a cup of tea to drink, and she was hungry too. But not for anything would she have faced the hostile looks of the other girls that afternoon. She had played so well – and won the match for her team – and if they couldn't even say "Well played!" she didn't want anything to do with them!

Miss Roberts noticed that Margery was missing. She guessed what had happened. She had heard all about the Big Row, and knew that Margery was being punished by the girls for her misbehaviour. Well – people always *were* punished for that kind of thing, by being

74

disliked. Miss Roberts could not do anything about it.

Erica's meanness had been almost forgotten in the excitement of the Big Row, and the match. But Erica had not forgotten that she meant to pay back Pat for finding out her trick, and punishing her for it. She had spent a good deal of time wondering how to get even with her. It was not so easy as it had seemed at first, because the two girls were in different forms.

But Erica soon found one or two things to do. She saw that Pat was making herself a red jumper, with which she was very pleased. She waited for her chance, and then, one evening when she saw that Pat had put the knitting back into her bag on the shelf, she made up her mind to spoil it.

There was a school meeting that evening. "If I go in late for it, I can sit at the back," thought Erica. "Then I can slip out half-way through for a few minutes, and come back without any one noticing. That will just give me time to get to the common room and back."

So that evening, at half-past seven, when the meeting had just begun, Erica slipped in at the back. No one noticed her, for Miss Walker was speaking, and every one was listening. Margery Fenworthy was at the back too. That was usually her place now – at the back for it was horrid to be anywhere where people had the chance of looking disdainfully at you! No one saw you if you sat at the back.

Erica sat for a while, listening. When Miss Walker sat down, and Miss Lewis got up to speak, Erica slipped out. No one saw her at all. She ran at top speed to the empty common room. She went to Pat's corner of the shelf and took down her knitting bag.

75

In it was the half-finished jumper, knitted most beautifully, for Pat was very proud of it. Erica took out the knitting and pulled the needles from the wool. She wrenched at the jumper, and half the even knitting came undone. Erica, with a feeling of real spite, tore at the wool again – and it broke in half a dozen places! The girl hurriedly pushed the knitting into the bag, and then ran back to the meeting. Miss Lewis was still speaking, in her clear, sharp tones.

No one saw Erica slip in – no one except Margery, who paid no attention, for she was lost in her own thoughts. Erica hugged herself secretly, pleased with what she had done. In her mean little soul she rejoiced that she had harmed some one who had brought her to justice.

The meeting finished. The girls yawned and stretched. Pat looked at her watch.

"Eight o'clock," she said. "Time for a game of something in the common room. Come on."

"There's dance music on the wireless," said Doris. "Let's put that on. I want to dance!"

"I've got some French to finish," groaned Sheila. "Blow! I wish I'd done it before. I daren't leave it. Mam'zelle always seems in such a bad temper these days."

"Yes, doesn't she," said Isabel, who had noticed the same thing. "I'm getting quite scared of her!"

They all went back to the common room. The third-formers went to the big room they shared with the fourth form, and the top-formers went to their studies. The time before bed was always cosy and friendly and jolly.

"What are you going to do, Isabel?" asked Pat. "Shall we finish that jigsaw puzzle Tessie lent us?"

"No," said Isabel. "I want to mend a stocking. I

76

shall have Matron after me if I don't. She told me to do it three days ago and I forgot."

"All right. I'll talk to you and knit," said Pat, reaching up to the shelf for her bag. "I'm getting on so well with my red jumper. I can't imagine what Mother will say when she sees it! I've never stuck at knitting so long before."

"Let's see what it looks like," said Janet, coming up. Pat took out her knitting and undid it. The needles dropped to the floor. The wool hung torn and unravelled.

"Pat!" gasped Isabel, in horror. "Pat! It's all undone! It's spoilt!"

"Gracious goodness!" said Janet, taking a glance at Pat's horrified face as she saw her ruined work. "Who's done that?"

"Oh, Pat – I'm so sorry about it," said Isabel, who knew what hard and careful work Pat had put into the jumper. "Oh, Pat – whatever *has* happened to it?"

Pat stared at her spoilt work. It was a shock to her, and she was near tears. She blinked hard and swallowed the lump that suddenly came into her throat.

"Somebody's done this to me," she said, in a low voice. "Somebody's done it to pay me out."

"Margery!" said Isabel, at once. "She overheard what you said about not clapping or cheering her in the match – and this is her way of paying you out. Oh, the mean, mean thing!"

Janet flushed with anger. She hated meanness of any kind. "Well, if she's done that, she'll jolly well have to be hauled up about it!" she said. "Look here, girls – come and look at Pat's knitting."

The first- and second-formers crowded round. Erica came too, pretending by be surprised and shocked. She was enjoying herself very much. If only nobody

77

guessed it was she who had done it!

But every one thought it was Margery. No one imagined it was Erica, for by now they had half-forgotten her mean behaviour. They crowded round Pat and sympathized with her.

"It *is* rotten luck," said Tessie. "I know what it feels like even to drop a stitch when you're trying to make something really nice. But to have it all spoilt and pulled out like that – and broken in so many places – that's dreadful. What will you do? Can you do anything about it?"

"I shall just have to undo it all and begin again, that's all," said Pat. It had given the girl a great shock to think that any one could play such a mean trick on her. Real spite is always horrible – and Pat had never come across it directed at herself before.

"Well, what are we going to do about Margery?" said Janet, fiercely. "She's got to be dealt with, hasn't she?"

"Where is she?" said Hilary. Just as she spoke Margery came into the room with a book. She had been to the school library to get it. Janet rounded on her at once.

"Margery! Come here! We've all seen your latest display of bad temper!"

Margery looked surprised. "What do you mean, Janet?" she asked, coldly.

"Oh, don't pretend like that!" said Janet. "Look here – do you dare to say you didn't do that to Pat's knitting?"

She held up the ruined jumper. Margery stared at it in amazement. "Of course I didn't," she said, with a queer dignity. "I'm bad-tempered and sulky, and there's not much that's good about me, according to all of you – but I don't do mean tricks like that. I dislike Pat, and I'd like to get even with her for some of the unkind things she's done to me – but not in that way."

The girls stared at her. Nobody believed her. Pat went red, and put the knitting back into her bag.

"You did do it, Margery, you know you did!" cried Isabel, quite beside herself because her twin had been hurt. "You must have slipped out whilst we were at the meeting and done it then!"

"No, I didn't," said Margery. "It's true I was at the back – but what's the good of being anywhere else when you all send me to Coventry, as you do? But I tell you quite honestly I didn't play that trick. I could *not* do a trick like that. I might slap Pat or box her ears, or slash her at lacrosse – but I wouldn't do a hole-and-corner thing like that."

"You'd do anything!" said Janet, scornfully. "I bet you wouldn't stick at anything once you got your knife into somebody!"

"You're just proving the truth of the old saying 'Give a dog a bad name and hang him,'" said Margery. "Because I'm bad in some things you think I'm capable of doing anything horrid. I'm not."

Her eyes suddenly filled with tears and she turned away to hide them. Tears were weak. She could not bear any one to see them. She walked out of the room and left a surprised and furious crowd behind her.

"Well, would you think *any*one would have the nerve to deny it like that?" demanded Kathleen.

"She's absolutely brazen!" declared Tessie.

"Oh, shut up about it," said Pat. "Let's not say any more. We can't prove it – and though we're all jolly sure she did it, it's no good going on and on about it. It's hateful, but it's best forgotten."

"Well, it's decent of you to feel like that," said Doris, going to the wireless. "I wish I knew exactly how and when she did it. Who'd like a little dance music to cheer us up?"

Soon the wireless was blaring out dance tunes and Doris and Janet were fox-trotting round the room, doing all sorts of ridiculous steps to make the others laugh. And the one who laughed the loudest was Erica.

"What luck!" she thought. "No one even thought of me – and they've pinned the blame on to Margery! Now I can think of something else to do to Pat, and nobody will imagine it's any one but that bad-tempered Margery!"

The Twins hear a Secret

That week-end was half-term. Most of the parents who could do so came by train to see their girls, or motored down to them. Those girls whose parents were not able to visit them either went out with their friends, or were taken into the next town to see a cinema or play.

Mrs. O'Sullivan came by car, and took Pat and Isabel, and also Alison, whose mother could not come. Janet went joyfully with her parents on a long picnic ride, and took Hilary with her. Margery's parent did not come at all – and no one asked her to go out with them, so she went with Miss Roberts and four other girls to see the cinema show in the next town.

Isabel was still full of how Pat's jumper had been ruined. She poured it all out to Mrs. O'Sullivan, and Alison chattered about it too. Pat said very little. She had been shocked and hurt by it, for she was a friendly girl and had had few enemies in her life.

Mrs. O'Sullivan listened. "You are quite sure that

Margery did it?" she asked. "Don't you think you ought to withhold your judgment until you are quite certain! There is nothing so dreadful as to accuse a person wrongly, you know. It makes them very bitter – and from what you tell me poor Margery must have already had some unhappiness of some sort in her life."

Mrs. O'Sullivan's remark made the three girls feel a little uncomfortable. They did feel sure that Margery had spoilt the jumper – but it was quite true that they hadn't any real proof.

No one said anything more – but privately Pat and Isabel decided to do as their mother said – and not judge Margery until they actually had some real proof. After all, although she was bad-tempered and rude, she had never shown before that she could be either mean or deceitful. Alison looked at the twins and thought she would do as they did – if they told her what that would be! Alison was getting a little better now and hadn't quite such a good opinion of herself.

But their good intentions were quite ruined by a chance meeting with an old friend of theirs that afternoon. They were having lunch in a big town some twenty miles away from the school, and afterwards were going to see a play there. And, having lunch at a nearby table was Pamela Holding, a girl who had been at Redroofs for a year or two whilst the twins had been there.

"Hallo, Pam!" cried Isabel, seeing her first. "Are you having half-term holiday too?"

"Hallo, Pat, hallo, Isabel – and is that Alison!" cried Pam. "Yes – I'm at school at St. Hilda's, and Mother is taking me to the play here this afternoon for my half-term treat. Don't say you're going too!"

"Well, we are!" said Pat, pleased. "Let's all go together, and have tea with one another afterwards."

The two mothers knew and liked each other, so they approved of this idea. The four girls and the two grown-ups set off to the theatre at half-past two, chattering and laughing, exchanging all their news.

Unfortunately their seats were not side by side in the theatre, so they had to part there – but arranged to meet for tea. And it was at tea that the twins heard some queer news about Margery Fenworthy.

Pamela was telling the twins and Alison about some one in her school who had just won the record for long distance running.

"Well, we've a girl at our school who could win any records she liked, I should think," said Alison. "She's just a miracle at games and gym. Her name's Margery Fenworthy."

"Margery Fenworthy!" said Pamela, her eyes opening wide. "You don't mean to tell me *she's* at St. Clare's! Golly! We all wondered where she'd gone."

"Why – was she at St. Hilda's with you last term then?" asked Pat, in surprise. "She never will say anything about the schools she has been to."

"No wonder," said Pamela, scornfully. "She's been to about six already!"

"Why so many?" asked Isabel in amazement.

"Can't you guess?" said Pam. "She's been expelled from the whole lot, as far as I can make out. I know that St. Hilda's stuck her for two terms – and then out she went! She was just too unbearable for words. So rude in class that no mistress would have her!"

The twins stared at Pamela. Yes – that was Margery all right! So she had been sent away from one school after another. What a disgrace!

"Good gracious!" said Alison, finding her tongue first. "Well, I should think she'll be sent away from St. Clare's soon too. Do you know what she did to Pat?"

And out came the whole history of the spoilt jumper – and then the story of the Big Row. Pamela listened, her eyes wide with interest.

"Well, I must say the Big Row sounds just exactly like Margery," she said. "I could tell you things that are more or less the same about her – but the affair of the jumper doesn't sound quite like Margery. I mean – she might in a temper snatch it out of Pat's hand and pull it to pieces in front of her – but as far as I know Margery never did anything behind anyone's back at St. Hilda's. She must be getting worse."

"What was she expelled from other schools for?" asked Alison, eagerly.

"Oh, bad temper – rudeness – insubordination they called it," said Pamela. "She wouldn't work at all at St. Hilda's. She's sixteen, you know. I bet she's only in your form, Pat and Isabel."

"Yes, she is," said Pat. "We thought she must be sixteen. Her work isn't even up to our form's, though. She is always bottom – when Alison isn't!"

Alison flushed. "Don't be mean!" she said. "I haven't been bottom for three weeks! I've been trying hard lately."

"All right, featherhead," said Pat, good humouredly. "I think you *have* been trying. Well – it's a race between you and Doris and Margery who'll be bottom the oftenest this term – so you'd better buck up and try a bit harder!"

The three cousins had plenty to talk about as they went back to school in the car. They sat at the back whilst Mrs. O'Sullivan drove.

"So Margery is sixteen!" said Isabel. "Golly, isn't

she a dunce? And fancy being expelled so many times! I wonder that St. Clare's took her."

Mrs. O'Sullivan chimed in expectedly. "If any school can help that miserable girl you keep talking about it should be St. Clare's. Miss Theobald prides herself on getting the best out of the worst – and I'm quite sure she knows all about Margery Fenworthy, and is hoping that St. Clare's will be the one school that will keep her."

The three girls were silent. Secretly they had all been hoping that there might be the excitement of Margery being expelled from St. Clare's too. But now the twins' mother had put the matter in rather a different light. It *would* be a score for St. Clare's if it could keep Margery.

"Mother – do you think we'd better not tell the other girls about Margery?" asked Pat, at last, voicing what the others had been thinking too.

"I certainly think there's no doubt about it," said Mrs. O'Sullivan. "Why should you spread tales about the girl, when, for all you know, she is simply dreading any one knowing her secret? You say she will not tell you what schools she has been to. She doesn't boast about being expelled – so she is evidently ashamed of it. She hasn't behaved well, but I think you shouldn't give her away."

The twins felt the same. Much as they disliked Margery they didn't want to spread round the news they had heard. But Alison was rather disappointed.

"It would have been such a bit of news!" she couldn't help saying.

"Now, Alison, if you start to bleat this all over the place –" began Pat, crossly, but Alison gave her a push.

"Be quiet! I shan't tell a soul. And will you STOP

84

saying I bleat? I just hate that word! I've tried not to bleat lately, but you just go on and on saying it."

Alison's eyes were full of the tears she could call up at a moment's notice. But Pat knew the girl was really upset, so she gave her a friendly pinch.

"Shut up, silly! I know you won't say a word. We can trust you all right, I know."

But although the three girls did not say a word to any one they could not help feeling that such a bad record was terrible – and they felt that Margery might be anything bad – she might be capable of doing the meanest, horridest things. Each of the girls believed she had ruined the jumper, and when any one said so in their hearing, they all agreed.

Margery took no notice of any one. She was always reading, and she did not seem to hear the remarks made by the girls in front of her. Her good-looking face was even more sullen than usual, and she was the despair of all the mistresses!

Erica Again

Erica was eagerly on the look-out for another trick to play on Pat or Isabel. If she could make it appear that it was done by Margery, so much the better!

But it was not very easy to play a trick without drawing attention to herself. She waited for a week, and then a chance put the opportunity in her way.

There was a nature-walk one afternoon. All the first- and second-formers had to go. They were to take their satchels with them, with their nature notebooks, and their tins for collecting specimens.

Miss Roberts and Miss Jenks were going too. The

woods were to be visited, and the ponds. There should be quite a lot of things to observe, draw and collect.

The twins were excited about the outing, which was to take up the whole of one afternoon. It was a brilliantly fine day and the sun was quite warm.

"There might be early tadpoles or frog-spawn in the ponds," said Pat. "I think I'll take a little jar in case."

All the girls prepared their satchels and put into them their nature books, their tins and jars. Pat was proud of her nature notebooks. She had done some beautiful drawings in them, and Miss Roberts had said they were good enough to be exhibited at the end of the term.

"I've just got one more page to fill," she said to Isabel. "I'll do it this afternoon. Are you ready? You're walking with me, aren't you?"

"Of course!" said Isabel. It was no good any one else asking to walk with either of the twins because they always went with each other. They preferred each other to any of the other girls, much as they liked Janet and Hilary and Lucy.

All the girls paired off. No one wanted to go with Erica or Margery, and so it came about that those two found themselves together. They did not like one another and walked in silence. Some of the girls nudged each other and giggled when they saw the silent pair.

"Two bad eggs together!" giggled Winnie. "I hope they're enjoying each other's conversation! Doesn't Margery's face look black – she's in one of her tempers, I expect."

Margery *was* feeling rather ill-tempered, for she had hoped to walk by herself. She did not like being paired off with the mean little Erica. So she said nothing, hoping that Erica would take the hint and leave her to herself as much as possible.

The afternoon went on happily in the yellow sunshine. The girls wandered over the woods, and made notes and sketches, and collected twigs and moss. Some of them found early primroses and stuck them into their button-holes.

Then they went down to the ponds, and exclaimed in surprise to see frog-spawn already floating at the top of the water.

"I *must* get some!" said Pat at once.

"You can't," said Isabel. "It's too far in. You'll get your shoes wet."

Pat took a quick glance round. "Where are Miss Roberts and Miss Jenks? Look – they're still at the top of the hill. I've time to take off my shoes and stockings and wade in!"

The girls giggled. "Pat, you do do some awful things!" said Janet. "Miss Roberts will *not* be pleased with you – and your feet will be as muddy as anything."

"Feet can be cleaned," said Pat. She took off her satchel and hung it on a post not far off. She took out her little jar and put it down on the bank. Then she stripped off her shoes and stockings and waded into the pond.

"Ooooo! The water's jolly cold!" she said. "And it's mud at the bottom – horrid! Oh – I've trodden on a snail or something!"

Pat made every one laugh. All the girls crowded round, laughing, watching her as she waded here and there.

She reached the frog-spawn and bent down to get it. It slipped through her fingers back into the pond. Isabel laughed.

"Try again, old girl!" she cried. Pat did her best to catch the slippery spawn, but time after time it slipped down into the water. Soon all the watching girls were

Everyone watched as Pat waded in the pond

in a state of giggle, and did not see Miss Roberts or Miss Jenks coming to the pond!

"Pat!" suddenly cried Miss Roberts's voice, in horror. "What in the world are you doing? Oh, you naughty girl – you'll get your death of cold, wading into the icy water like that! Come out at once!"

"Oh, Miss Roberts – please, Miss Roberts, let me get some frog-spawn first," begged Pat, snatching another handful, that promptly slithered between her fingers back into the pond again.

"Pat! *Will* you come out!" cried Miss Roberts. "Really, I can't leave you first-formers for a single minute!"

All the girls but two were watching the scene with the greatest interest and amusement. Those two were Erica and Margery. Margery had stayed behind in a field to watch some horses ploughing – and Erica had dawdled too.

Erica heard the laughter going on and hastened to see what the excitement was. Before she got to the pond she saw Pat's satchel hanging on to the post. On it was Pat's name – P. O'Sullivan.

Erica took a quick look at the pond. Not a single girl was looking her way. Anyway, she was out of sight, behind the hedge. She looked to see where Margery was. But Margery was still up in the field, watching the horses.

Quick as lightning Erica took the satchel off the post and opened it. Down into the mud she flung all Pat's precious nature books, and her tins of nature finds. She ground the books into the mud with her heel and stamped on the tins.

She flung the satchel into the hedge. Then, as silently as she could, she ran behind the hedge and came up to the pond from the opposite direction. No one noticed her. When Tessie saw her there she imagined that Erica had been there all the time.

Pat was wading out of the water. Her feet were terribly cold. She took out her handkerchief and dried them, and Miss Roberts slapped them well to get the circulation back. Then she made Pat put on her shoes and stockings and run up the hill and back to warm herself.

"And after all that I didn't get any frog-spawn!" said Pat, sorrowfully, as she rejoined the others, her feet tingling. "Where's my satchel? Where did I put it?"

"Over there on the post," said Isabel, turning to point. But the satchel wasn't there.

"Well, that's funny," said Isabel. "I saw you put it there. Look – there's Margery nearby. Margery! Bring Pat's satchel over with you if you can see it."

"What's that in the hedge?" suddenly said Shelia, pointing. Her sharp eyes had seen the big brown satchel there.

"Golly! It's my satchel!" said Pat, in astonishment. "How did it get there?"

She ran to get it – and then saw the note-books stamped down into the mud – and the dented tins with their little collections spilt on the ground. She said nothing, but there was something in her face that made the girls run towards her.

"What's up, Pat?" asked Isabel – and then she too saw what had happened. There was absolutely no doubt at all but that some spiteful hand had done the mischief. There was the half-imprint of a muddy foot on the exercise book – and some one had stamped on the tins!

"It – it couldn't have been a cow or something,

90

could it?" said Isabel, hating to think that some one had done this to her twin.

Janet shook her head. "No, of course not. I think we all know who did it – though we didn't see."

All the girls looked at Margery, who was standing nearby, looking as surprised as the others. "Who was the only one not at the pond?" said Janet. "Margery! Why did she stay behind? To play this beastly trick, I suppose!"

"Girls! What is the matter?" asked Miss Roberts, coming up. "Oh, Pat – are those your books in the mud? How careless! And all your beautiful drawings spoilt too. How did that happen?"

"I don't know, Miss Roberts," said Poor Pat, red with dismay. She could not bring herself to sneak on Margery, even at that moment. Miss Roberts saw that something serious was the matter, and could hear Margery's name being whispered around her.

"Well, pick up your things quickly," said Miss Roberts, looking at her watch. "You have made us late with your paddling. Hurry now. This matter can be settled later on."

The girls walked quickly home. Erica had to walk with Margery. She was pleased that her mean trick had come off so well, and that Margery had once again been blamed for what was not her fault. Margery walked as if she was in a dream. She simply could not understand who had done these things, for she knew quite well that *she* had not! Who could be so amazingly mean as to do them – and let some one else take the blame? Not even Erica, surely!

She took a glance at Erica, walking by her side. There was something in the smug look on the girl's face that made Margery begin to suspect her. She remembered suddenly how she had noticed Erica slipping back into the meeting the night the jumper was spoilt. *Could* it be Erica! She was a mean little sneak – every one knew it – but could she be so hateful as that?

"Well, it's some one," thought Margery, bitterly, "and as usual I get all the blame. What an unlucky creature I am!"

That evening after tea the girls talked about the latest trick on poor Pat. Margery could not bear their scornful glances and went to the school library to pretend to choose a book.

And whilst she was there Alison let the cat out of the bag!

"We didn't mean to tell this," she began, looking all round, "but now that we've seen this fresh bit of spite from Margery, I'm going to tell you all a bit of interesting news."

"Shut up, Alison," said Pat.

"I'm not going to shut up," said Alison, with spirit. "Do you think I'm going to stand by and see these things happen without getting back on Margery if I can? Now just you listen everybody!"

All the girls were silent, listening eagerly. What *could* Alison be going to tell them?

"We met an old friend of ours at half-term," said Alison. "She goes to St. Hilda's – and Margery went there – and she was expelled from there!"

There was a buzz of horror. Expelled! What a dreadful disgrace! And to think she was at St. Clare's! No wonder she would never say what school she had been to!

"Not only that," went on Alison, her eyes flashing round, "but she has been to five or six schools altogether – and has been sent away from each one! Do you wonder she's backward? Do you wonder she's still in the first form when she's *sixteen*!"

A loud chatter broke out. The girls were amazed. They couldn't believe it – and yet it was so easy to believe, knowing Margery!

"Well, why should *St. Clare's* have to have her!" cried Tessie, in indignation. "Why have *we* got to put up with her, I'd like to know?"

"Turn her out!" cried Hilary.

"Let's go to Miss Theobald and say we don't want to have a girl like that here!" cried Winnie.

"My mother wouldn't let me stay here if she knew there was a girl like Margery here!" said Erica.

"You be quiet," said Tessie, giving Erica a push. She wasn't going to let mean little Erica give herself airs.

"Well, now we know all about dear Margery!" said Doris. "The girl who has been expelled from six schools – and will soon be expelled from the seventh! And a jolly good thing too. She won't be able to wreak her spite on Pat any more."

There was a sound at the door. The girls turned. Margery was there, as white as chalk. She had heard what Doris had said, and was fixed to the spot with horror. So her poor secret was out. She didn't know how the girls had learnt it – but evidently some one had found out about her. And now she would have to leave St. Clare's.

Margery stared at the girls out of her deep brown eyes. She opened her mouth to say something but no words came. She turned round and left the silent girls there; they heard her footsteps tip-tapping uncertainly along the passage.

"Well, we've done it now!" said Isabel, feeling rather scared. "The secret's out – and the whole school will know tomorrow!"

Margery makes a Discovery

The twins felt most uncomfortable about Margery. Yet they could not blame their cousin for telling the girl's secret. Alison had been very indignant about the trick that had been played on Pat, and it was her way of backing up her cousin, to talk against Margery.

"I say – you don't think Margery will run away or anything like that, do you?" said Pat, to Isabel. "You know, Isabel – if that sort of thing happened to me, I couldn't stay one moment more at St. Clare's. I simply couldn't. I'd have to go home."

"Maybe Margery hasn't much of a home to go to," said Isabel. "You know, she never talks about her home as we all do – she never says anything about her mother and father, or if she had any brothers or sisters. Does she? It seems rather queer to me."

"I don't think we can leave things like this," said Lucy Oriell, looking grave. "I think Miss Theobald must have known all about Margery – and her bad reputation – and I think she must have said she would let her try here, at St. Clare's. And I think something else too – I think that all the mistresses were in the secret, and knew about Margery – and that they have been asked to be lenient with her to give her a chance."

The girls stared at Lucy's serious little face. She was such a sweet-natured girl that every one listened to her willingly. No one had ever known Lucy say anything horrid about any one.

"I think you're right, Lucy," said Pat. "I've often wondered why Margery seemed to get away with rudeness and carelessness – whilst we got into hot water if we did the same things. I knew of course it wasn't favouritism, for no mistress could possibly *like* Margery. Now I understand."

"Yes – Lucy's right," said Hilary. "All the mistresses were in the secret, and were trying to help Margery, hoping she'd turn over a new leaf, and be all right at St. Clare's. What a hope!"

"It's this meanness I can't stand," said Pat. "I can put up with bad manners and rudeness and even sulkiness, but I just hate meanness."

"Yes, I agree with you there," said Janet. "You can't do much with a mean nature. Well – what are we going to do about Margery? Lucy, you said we couldn't leave things as they are now. What do you suggest doing?"

"I suggest that we all sleep on it, and then one or more of us should go to Miss Theobald tomorrow and tell all we know," said Lucy. "If Margery can't face us after what has happened, then she ought to be given the chance to go. But if she still wants to stay, and face it out, then she ought to have the chance to do that. But Miss Theobald ought to decide – not us. We don't know enough. Miss Theobald probably knows the reason for Margery's funny behaviour. We don't."

"All right. Let's sleep on it," said Janet. "My mother always says that's a good thing to do. Things often seem different after a night's sleep. Well – we'll do that – and tomorrow we'll go to Miss Theobald and tell her all we know."

"Lucy must go," said Hilary. "She's good at that sort of thing. She's got no spite in her and can tell a story fairly. Pat and Isabel had better go too – because after all, it's against Pat that these hateful tricks have been directed."

"All right," said Lucy. "I'd rather *not* go really, because I hate being mixed up in this sort of thing. But somebody's got to go. Well, that's decided then."

But although the girls had laid their plans seriously and carefully, they were not to be put into action. For something happened that night that upset them completely, and that changed everything in a few hours.

The girls all went to bed as usual. Erica had complained of a sore throat and had been sent to Matron. Matron had taken her temperature, and found that it was a hundred. So into the sanatorium went Erica, where two other girls were, with bad chills.

"You've just got a chill too," said Matron. "Now drink this, and settle down quickly into bed. I'll pop in and see you later. You'll probably be normal tomorrow, and can go back to school the next day if you're sensible."

Erica didn't mind at all. She rather liked missing lessons for a day or two – and she felt that it was lucky to be away when all the fuss was being made about Margery. Erica was a mean soul – but even she had been horrified at the look on Margery's face when she had overheard what the girls were saying about her.

"I wouldn't have played those tricks and made it seem as if they'd been done by Margery if I'd known the girls were going to find out about her being expelled – and blame the tricks on to her as well as despise her for her disgrace," thought Erica, her conscience beginning to prick her for the first time. "I wish I hadn't done them now. But I do hate that horrid Pat. It does serve her right to have her jumper spoilt and all her nature books!"

Erica got undressed and into bed. She was alone in a little room at the top of the sanatorium, which was a separate building on the west side of the school. In the san. were put any infectious cases, any girls with

96

measles and so on, or who had perhaps sprained an ankle. Here Matron looked after them and kept them under her eye until they were well enough to go back to their forms.

Erica was put into a room alone because Matron was not quite sure if her cold was going to turn to something infectious. There had been a case of measles among the Oakdene girls who had played the match against St. Clare's, and the mistresses had been on the watch in case any of their own girls should have caught it from the Oakdene girl.

So Erica was not put with the two girls who had chills, in case by any chance she was beginning measles, which she hadn't had.

It was a nice little room, well-tucked away at the top of the san. Erica looked out of the window before she got into bed and saw a sky full of stars. She drew back the curtains so that the sun could come in the next morning and then got into bed.

Matron came along with a hot-water bottle and some hot lemon and honey. Erica enjoyed it. Then Matron tucked her up, switched off the light, and left her to go to sleep.

Erica was soon asleep. Her conscience did not keep her awake, for it was not a very lively one. If Pat or Isabel had done the things that Erica had done lately, neither of them would have been able to sleep at night because of feeling mean and wretched. But Erica went sweetly off to sleep, and slept as soundly as any of the girls in her form.

But one girl did not sleep that night. It was Margery. She lay in her dormitory, wide awake, thinking of what she had heard the girls say about her. Always, always, wherever she went, her secret was found out, and sooner or later she had to go. She didn't want to be at school. She didn't want to stay at home. She wished with all her might that she could go out into the world and find a job and earn her own living. It was dreadful going from school to school like this, getting worse every time!

The other girls slept soundly. Someone snored a little. Margery turned over to her left side and shut her eyes. If only she could go to sleep! It only she could stop thinking and thinking! What was going to happen tomorrow? Now that all the girls knew about her, things would be terrible.

She couldn't go home. She couldn't run away because she only had a few shillings. There was simply nothing she could do but stay and be miserable – and when she was miserable she didn't care about anything in the world, and that made her rude and careless and sulky.

"There isn't any way out for me," thought the girl. "There's simply nothing I can do. If only there was something – some way of escape from all this. But there isn't."

She turned over on to her right side, and shut her eyes again. But in a moment they were wide open. It was impossible to go to sleep. She tried lying on her back, staring up into the dark. But that didn't make her sleepy either. She heard the school clock chime out. Eleven o'clock. Twelve o'clock. One o'clock. Two o'clock. Was there ever such a long night as this? At this rate the night would never be over.

"I'll get myself a drink of water," said Margery, sitting up. "Maybe that will help me to go to sleep."

She put on her dressing-gown and slippers and found her torch. She switched it on. Its light showed her the sleeping forms of the other girls. No one stirred as she went down between the cubicles to the door.

She opened the door and went out into the passage. There was a bathroom not far off, with glasses. She went there and filled a glass with water. She took it to the window to drink it.

And it was whilst she was standing there, drinking the icy-cold water that she saw something that puzzled her. She forgot to finish the water, and set the glass down to peer out of the window.

The bathroom window faced the sanatorium, which was a four-storey building, tall and rather narrow. It was in complete darkness except at one place.

A flickering light showed now and again from high up on the third storey. It came from a window there. Margery puzzled over it. She tried to think what it could be.

"It looks like flickering firelight," she thought. "But who is sleeping on the third storey, I wonder? Wait a minute – surely that isn't the window of a bedroom? Surely it's the little window that gives light to the stair-way that goes up to the top storey?"

She watched for a little while, trying to make certain. But in the darkness she couldn't be sure if it was the staircase window or a bedroom window. The light flickered on and on, exactly as if it were the glow of a bedroom fire, sometimes dancing up into flames and sometimes dying down.

"I'd better go back to bed," said Margery to herself, shivering. "It's probably the room where Erica is – and Matron has given her a fire in her bedroom for a treat. It's the flickering glow I can see."

So back to bed she went – but she kept worrying a little about that curious light – and in the end she got out of bed once more to see if it was still there.

And this time, looking out of the bathroom window, she knew without any doubt what it was. It was Fire, Fire, Fire!

A Wonderful Rescue

As soon as Margery saw the light for the second time, she gave a shout. The whole of the staircase window was lighted up, and flames were shooting out of it!

"Fire!" yelled Margery, and darted off to Miss Roberts's room. She hammered on her door.

"Miss Roberts! Miss Roberts! Quick, come and look! The san. is on fire! Oh, quick!"

Miss Roberts woke with a jump. Her room faced on to the san. and she saw at once what Margery had just seen. Dragging on a dressing-gown she ran to the door. Margery clutched hold of her.

"Miss Roberts! Shall I go across and see if Matron knows! I'm sure she doesn't!"

"Yes, run quickly!" said Miss Roberts. "Don't wake any of the girls in this building, Margery – there's no need for them to know. Hurry now. I'll get Miss Theobald and we'll join you."

Margery tore down the stairs and undid the side door. She raced across the piece of grass that separated the san. from the school. She hammered on the door there and shouted.

"Matron! Matron! Are you there!"

Matron was fast asleep on the second floor. She didn't wake. It was Queenie, one of the girls in bed with a chill who heard Margery shouting. She ran to the window and looked out.

"What is it, what is it?" she cried.

"The san. is on fire!" shouted Margery. "Flames are coming out on the storey above you. Wake Matron!"

The girl darted into the Matron's room. She shook her hard, calling to her in fright. Matron woke up in a hurry and pulled on a coat.

Miss Theobald appeared with some of the other mistresses. Some one had telephoned for the fire-engine. Girls appeared from everywhere, in spite of mistresses' orders to go back to bed.

"Good gracious! Go back to bed when there's a perfectly good fire on!" said Janet, who, as usual, was eager to enjoy any experience that came her way.

"Golly, I've never seen a fire before! I'm going to enjoy this one. Nobody's in any danger!"

Girls swarmed all over the place. Matron tried to find the three who had had chills – Queenie, Rita, and Erica. "They mustn't stand about in this cold night air, she said, very worried. "Oh, there you are, Queenie. You are to go at once to the second-form dormitory and get into the first bed you see there. Is Rita with you – and where is Erica?"

"Rita's here," said Queenie, "and I think I saw Erica somewhere."

"Well, find her and take her to bed at once," ordered Matron. "Where are the two maids? Are they safe?"

Yes – they were safe. They were shivering in their coats nearby, watching the flames getting bigger and bigger.

"Matron, is every one out of the sanatorium?" asked Miss Theobald. "Are you sure? All the girls? The maids? Any one else?"

"I've seen Queenie," said Matron, "and Rita – and Queenie said she saw Erica. Those are the only girls

101

I had in. And the two maids are out. They are over there."

"Well, that's all right then," said Miss Theobald, in relief. "Oh, I wish that fire-engine would hurry up. I'm afraid the fourth storey will be completely burnt out."

Queenie had not seen the right Erica. She *had* seen a girl called Erica, who was in the fourth form, and she had not known that Matron meant Erica of the second-form. Erica was still in the san.

No one knew this at all until suddenly Mam'zelle gave a scream and pointed with a trembling hand to the window of the top storey.

"Oh, que c'est terrible!" she cried. "There is some one there!"

Poor Erica was at the window. She had been awakened by the smell of smoke, and had found her bedroom dark with the evil-smelling smoke that crept in under and around her door. Then she had heard the crackling of the flames.

In a terrible fright she had jumped up and tried to switch on her light. But nothing happened. The wires outside had been burnt and there was no light in her room. The girl felt for her torch and switched it on.

She ran to the door – but when she opened it a great roll of smoke unfolded itself and almost choked her. There was no way out down the staircase. It was in flames.

The fire had been started by an electric wire which had smouldered on the staircase, and had kindled the dry wood nearby. The staircase was old and soon burnt fiercely. There was no way out for Erica. She tried to run into the next room, from whose window there was a fire-escape – but the smoke was so thick that it choked her and she had to run back into her own room.

102

She shut the door and rushed to the window.

She threw it open, and thankfully breathed in the pure night air. "Help!" she shouted, in a weak voice. "Help!"

No one heard her – but Mam'zelle saw her. Every one looked up at Mam'zelle's shout, and a deep groan went up as they saw Erica at the window.

Miss Theobald went pale, and her heart beat fast. A girl up there! And the staircase burning!

"The fire-engine isn't here," she groaned. "If only we had the fire-escape to run up its ladder to that high window! Oh, when will it come?"

Some one had found the garden-hose and was playing water on the flames. But the force of water was feeble and made little difference to the fire. Erica shouted again.

"Help! Save me! Oh, save me!" She could see all the crowd of people below and she could not think why some one did not save her. She did not realize that the fire-engine had not yet come, and that there was no ladder long enough to reach her.

"Where is the long garden ladder?" cried Margery, suddenly, seeing a gardener nearby. "Let's get it. Maybe we can send a rope up or something, even if the ladder isn't long enough!"

The men ran to get the longest ladder. They set it up against the wall and one of them ran up to the top. But it did not nearly reach Erica's window.

"It's no good," he said, when he came down. "It's impossible to reach. Where's that fire-engine? It's a long time coming."

"It's been called out to another fire," said one of the mistresses, who had just heard the news. "It's coming immediately."

"Immediately!" cried Margery. "Well, that's not

soon enough! Erica will soon be trapped by the flames."

Before any one could stop her the girl threw off her dressing-gown and rushed to the ladder. She was up it like a monkey, though Miss Theobald shouted to her to come back.

"You can't do anything, you silly girl!" cried the Head Mistress. "Come down!"

Every one watched Margery as she climbed to the very top of the ladder. The flames lighted up the whole scene now, and the dark figure of the climbing girl could be clearly seen.

"What *does* she think she can do?" said Miss Roberts, in despair. "She'll fall!"

But Margery had seen something that had given her an idea. To the right side of the ladder ran an iron pipe. Maybe she could swarm up that and get to Erica's window. What she was going to do then she didn't know – but she meant to do *some*thing!

She reached the top of the ladder. She put out a hand and caught hold of the strong iron pipe hoping that it was well nailed to the wall. Fortunately it was. Margery swung herself from the ladder to the pipe, clutching hold of it with her knees, and holding for dear life with her hands.

And now all her training in the gym stood her in good stead. All the scores of times she had climbed the ropes there had strengthened her arms and legs, and made them very steady and strong. It was far more difficult to climb an unyielding pipe than to swarm up a pliant rope, but Margery could do it. Up the pipe she went, pulling herself by her arms, and clinging with her knees and feet. Erica saw her coming.

"Oh, save me!" cried the girl, almost mad with fright. Margery came up to the window. Now was the

104

most difficult part. She had to get safely from the pipe to the window-sill.

"Erica! Hold on to something and give me a hand!" yelled Margery, holding out her hand above the window-sill. "If you can give me a pull I can get there."

Erica gave her hand to Margery. She held on to a heavy book-case just inside the room, and Margery swung herself strongly across to the sill from the pipe. She put up a knee, grazing it badly on the sill, but she did not even feel the pain. In half a moment she was inside the room. Erica clung to her, weeping.

"Now don't be silly," said Margery, shaking herself free and looking round the room, filled with dense black smoke. The flames were already just outside the door and the floor felt hot to her feet. "There's no time to lose. Where's your bed?"

Erica pointed through the smoke to where her bed was. Margery ran to it, choking, and dragged the sheets and blankets off it. She ran back to the window, and leaned her head outside to get some fresh air. Then she quickly tore the sheets in half.

"Oh, what are you doing?" cried Erica, thinking that Margery was quite mad. "Take me out of the window with you!"

"I will in a moment," said Margery, as she knotted the sheet-strips firmly together. There were four long strips. Margery looked for something to tie one end to. As she looked, the door fell in with a crash, and flames came into the room.

"Oh, quick, quick!" cried Erica. "I shall jump!"

"No, you won't," said Margery. "You're going to be saved – and very quickly too. Look here – see how I've knotted this sheet – and tied it to the end of your bed. Help me to drag the bed to the window. That's right."

Margery threw the other end of the sheet-strips out of the window. The end almost reached the top of the ladder! There was no need to climb down the pipe this time!

Margery sat herself on the window-sill and made Erica come beside her. Below, the crowds of girls and mistresses were watching what was happening, hardly daring to breathe. One of the gardeners had gone up the ladder, hoping to help.

"Now do you think you can climb down this sheet-rope I've made?" said Margery to the trembling Erica. "Look – it should be quite easy."

"Oh, no, I can't, I can't," sobbed Erica, terrified. So Margery did a very brave thing. She took Erica on her back, and with the frightened girl clinging tightly to her, her arms holding fast, she began to climb down the sheet-rope herself. Luckily the sheets were new and strong, and they held well.

Down went Margery and down, her arms almost pulled out of their sockets with Erica's weight. She felt with her feet for the ladder, and oh, how thankful she was when at last she felt the top rung, and a loud voice cried, "Well done, miss! I've got you!"

The gardener at the top of the ladder reached for Erica, and took hold of her. He helped the weeping girl down, and Margery slid down the few remaining feet of the sheet-rope.

What happened next nobody ever knew. It was likely that Margery was tired out with her amazing climb and equally amazing rescue, and that her feet slipped on the ladder – for somehow or other she lost her balance, and half slid, half fell down the ladder. She fell on the gardener, who helped to break her fall a little – but then she slid right off the ladder to the ground seven or eight feet below.

People rushed over to her – but Margery lay still. She had struck her head against something and was quite unconscious. Careful hands carried her into the big school just as the fire-engine rumbled up with a great clangour of its big bell. In one minute strong jets of water were pouring on to the flames, and in five minutes the fire was under control.

But the top storey, as Miss Theobald had feared, was entirely burnt out. The room where Erica had been sleeping was a mass of black charred timbers.

The girls were ordered back to bed, and this time they went! But there was one name on every one's lips that night – the name of a real heroine.

"Margery! Wasn't she wonderful! She saved Erica's life. Fancy her climbing that pipe like that. Let's pray she isn't much hurt. Margery! Well, wasn't she *wonderful!*"

A Confession

The next morning every one wanted to know how Margery was. A few remembered to ask about poor Erica, but it was Margery that people worried about.

"She's broken her leg! Poor old Margery! And she's hurt her head too, but not very badly. She's in the dressing-room off Miss Theobald's own bedroom. Miss Theobald is terribly pround of her!"

"I don't wonder!" said Janet, who always intensely admired bravery of any sort. "I don't care now what Margery has been like for the past few weeks. I've forgotten it all! A girl who can do a big thing like that can be as rude and sulky as she likes, for all I care!"

"And now I find it more difficult than ever to think

107

that Margery can have played any mean tricks!" said Lucy. "I simply can't help thinking we made a mistake over that. It *must* have been some one else! Courage of the sort that Margery showed last night never goes with a mean nature – never, never, never! It's impossible."

"I wish we knew for certain," said Alison, who was now feeling very guilty because she had told Margery's secret, and had let the girls know that she had been expelled from so many schools.

They did know, very soon, who was the guilty one. It was Lucy who found out. She went to see Erica who was in a little room off one of the dormitories, not much the worse for her adventure except that she was very sorry for herself.

Something had happened to Erica besides the fire. She had lain awake all that night, thinking of it – and thinking of Margery, who had rescued her.

And her conscience had come very much alive! To think that the girl who had so bravely saved her life was the girl who had been taking the blame for Erica's own meanness! Erica's cheeks burned when she thought of it. She wished it had been any other girl but Margery who had rescued her.

Lucy came to see her at the end of morning school. Nobody had been allowed to see Margery, who was to be kept quite quiet for a few days. No one had wanted very much to see Erica – but kind-hearted Lucy, as usual, thought of the girl lying alone in the little room, and asked Matron if she could see her.

"Yes, of course," said Matron. "She's normal this morning and there's nothing wrong with her except a bit of a cold and shock. It will do her good to see you."

So Lucy went into the little room and sat down

beside Erica. They talked for a while, and then Erica asked about Margery. She did not look at Lucy as she asked, for she felt very guilty.

"Haven't they told you about Margery?" said Lucy, in surprise. "Oh, poor thing, she's broken her right leg. That means no more gym or games for her for some time – and as they are the only things she cares about, she's going to have a pretty thin time. She hit her head on something too, but not very badly. She *was* a heroine, Erica!"

Erica was terribly upset. She had thought that Margery was quite all right, and had pictured her receiving the praise of the whole school. And now after all she was in bed with a broken leg and a bad head!

Erica turned her face to the wall, trying to think the matter out. She looked so miserable that Lucy was touched. She didn't like Erica, but misery of any kind must be comforted.

She took Erica's hand. "Don't worry about it," she said. "Her leg will mend – and she will be quite all right again. We are all very proud of her."

"Do you – do you still think she did those mean things?" asked Erica, not looking at Lucy.

"No, I don't," said Lucy at once. "Those kind of tricks don't go with a strong and fearless nature like Margery's. She's got plenty of faults – and bad ones too – but she has no petty, mean faults, as far as I can see."

Matron popped her head round the door. "Come along now, Lucy," she said. "Your ten minutes is up."

"Oh, don't go yet, don't go yet!" said Erica, clutching Lucy's hand, and feeling that she did not want to be left alone with her own thoughts. But Lucy had to go.

And then Erica had a very bad time indeed. It is hard enough when any one thinks contemptuously of us – but far worse if we have to despise ourselves. And that is what poor Erica found herself doing. She saw herself clearly – a mean, small, spiteful little creature, insincere and dishonest, and she didn't like herself at all.

She turned her face to the wall. She would not eat any dinner at all, and Matron took her temperature, feeling worried. But it was still normal.

"Are you worrying about something?" she asked. Erica's eyes filled with tears at the kind voice.

"Yes," she said desperately. "I'm worrying terribly. I can't stop."

"Tell me all about it," said Matron, gently.

"No," said Erica, and turned her face to the wall again. But she knew she could not keep all her thoughts to herself much longer. She had to tell some one, she simply had to. She called to Matron as she was going out of the room.

"Matron! I want Lucy!"

"My dear child, she's in class!" said Matron. "She can come and see you at tea-time, if you like."

Erica burst into floods of tears, and sobbed so heart-rendingly that Matron hurried over to her.

"Whatever *is* the matter?" she said.

"Matron, fetch Lucy," sobbed Erica. "Oh, do fetch Lucy."

Matron went out of the room and sent some one for Lucy. There was something queer about Erica's face, and the sooner she told somebody what was worrying her, the better! Lucy came along in surprise.

"Erica has something on her mind, Lucy," said Matron. "Try to get her to tell you, will you? Her

110

temperature will shoot up and she'll be really ill if she goes on like this."

Lucy went into the little room and sat down on Erica's bed. Erica had stopped crying, and her face was white and pinched. She stared dry-eyed at Lucy.

"What's up, old girl?" asked Lucy, her kind little face glowing with friendliness.

"Lucy! I've got to tell somebody or I'll go quite mad!" said Erica, desperately. "*I* did all those awful things to Pat. It wasn't Margery. It was me."

"Oh, Erica!" said Lucy, deeply shocked. "Poor, poor Margery!"

Erica said nothing. She turned her face to the wall again and lay still. She felt ill.

Lucy sat for a moment, taking in what Erica had said. Then, with an effort, she took Erica's cold hand. She knew that she must try to be kind to the girl, though she could hardly bring herself to be, because of her pity for what Margery must have gone through.

"Erica! I'm glad you told me. You know that I must tell the others, don't you? We mustn't for one moment more think that Margery did those things. We have accused her most unjustly, and treated her very unfairly. You see that I must tell the others, don't you?"

"Must you?" said Erica, her eyes filling with tears again. "But how can I face them all, if you do?"

"I don't know, Erica," said Lucy. "That's for you to decide. You have been awfully mean and spiteful. Why don't you tell Miss Theobald, now that you've told me, and see what she says?"

"No. I daren't tell her," said Erica, trembling as she thought of Miss Theobald's stern face. "You tell her, Lucy. Oh, Lucy – I want to leave here. I've done so badly. Nobody has ever liked me much – and nobody will ever, ever like me now. And there won't be a

111

chance for me to try properly if nobody feels friendly towards me. I'm a coward, you know. I can't stand up to things."

"I know," said Lucy gravely. "But sooner or later, you'll have to learn to face things that come along, Erica, and you'll have to get that meanness and spite out of your character, or you'll never be happy. I'll see Miss Theobald. Now don't worry too much. I'm very glad you told me all you did."

Lucy left Erica to her thoughts. She went to Matron. "Matron," she said, "Erica has told me what's worrying her – but it's something I ought to tell Miss Theobald. Can I go now?"

"Of course," said Matron, thinking that Lucy Oriell was one of the nicest girls who had ever come to St. Clare's. "Hurry along now. I'll send a message to Miss Roberts for you."

And so it came about that Lucy went to Miss Theobald with Erica's guilty secret, and related it all to the Head Mistress in her clear, friendly little voice. Miss Theobald listened gravely, not interrupting her at all.

"So Margery was accused wrongly," she said. "Poor Margery! She is a most unlucky child! But she did behave amazingly last night. What a plucky girl she is! She has two sides to her character – and the finer side came out very strongly yesterday."

"Miss Theobald, we know that Margery has been expelled from many schools," said Lucy, looking the Head straight in the eyes. "And we have guessed that the mistresses have been asked to be lenient with her to give her a chance at St. Clare's. And although I'm a new girl too I do see that any girl with a bad record would have a fine chance here to do better, because there's a wonderful spirit in this school. I've felt it and loved it. I'm so very glad my parents chose this school to send me to."

Miss Theobald looked at Lucy's honest and sincere face. She smiled one of her rare sweet smiles.

"And I too am glad that your parents sent you here," she said. "You are the type of girl that helps to make the spirit of the school a living powerful thing, Lucy."

Lucy flushed with pleasure, and felt very happy. Miss Theobald went back to the matter they had been discussing.

"Now we have to decide one or two things," she said, and at that word "we", Lucy felt proud and delighted. To think that she and Miss Theobald together were going to decide things!

"About Margery. You shall go and see her and tell her what you have told me. She must know as soon as possible that you have all been wrong about her, and that you know it and are sorry. She must know it was Erica too. How strange that girl she rescued should be the girl who did her so much wrong! Erica must have felt very upset about it."

"This will make a great difference to Margery," said Lucy, her eyes shining. "Every one will think of her as a heroine now, instead of as a sulky, rude girl. What a chance for Margery!"

"Yes – I think things may be easier for her now," said Miss Theobald. "You may have guessed that Margery's home is not quite a normal one, Lucy, and that has made things hard for her. I can't tell you any more. You must just be content with that! And now – what about Erica?"

They looked at one another gravely, and Lucy felt pride swell up in her as she saw how Miss Theobald trusted her opinion.

"Miss Theobald – things won't be easier for Erica," said Lucy. "She's awfully weak, you know. She won't be able to stand up to the girls' unfriendliness after this. If she only could, it would be the making of her. But I'm quite sure she can't. I think it would be better for her to go away and start all over again at another school. I don't mean expel her in disgrace – but couldn't something be arranged?"

"Yes, of course," said the Head Mistress. "I can explain things to her mother – she has no father, you know – and suggest that Erica goes home for the rest of the term, and then is sent to a fresh school in the summer – perhaps with the determination to do a great deal better! Poor Erica! What a good thing she at least had the courage to tell you."

Lucy left the Head Mistress feeling contented. It was good to know that some one wise and kindly had the handling of matters such as these. By this time it was teatime and Lucy went to the dining-hall feeling terribly hungry.

"Where *have* you been?" cried a dozen voices, as she came in. "You missed painting – and you love that!"

"Oh, dear – so I did!" said Lucy, sadly. "I forgot about that. Well – I couldn't help it."

"But, Lucy, where have you been and what have you been doing?" asked Pat. "Do tell us! You look all excited somehow."

"I've heard some interesting things," said Lucy, helping herself to bread and butter and jam. "I'll tell you in the common room after tea. I'm too hungry to talk now. You must just wait!"

The first- and second-formers crowded into their common room after tea, eager to hear what Lucy had to say. They knew quite well it was something exciting.

Lucy sat on a table and told them everything in her clear, calm voice. There were many interruptions, for the girls were intensely angry when they heard that it was Erica who had spoilt Pat's jumper and books – and had allowed the blame to rest on Margery.

"The beast! The hateful beast!"

"I'd like to pull all her hair out! I do feel a mean pig to think I blamed poor old Margery!"

"Oh, the spiteful creature! I'll never speak to her again as long as I live!"

"Just wait till she comes back into class! I'll give her an awful time. And to think that Margery broke her leg rescuing *that* mean creature!"

"Now listen," said Lucy, trying to stop the yells and shouts. "Do LISTEN! I've got something else to say."

Every one was quiet. Lucy then told them that Erica was to go home – not to be expelled in disgrace, but simply to go home and start again somewhere else. "And let's hope she's learnt her lesson and won't be quite so mean in future," said Lucy.

"She'd learn her lesson all right if only Miss Theobald made her come back into class," said Janet grimly.

"Yes, but she'd learn it in the wrong way," argued Lucy. "She'd just be scared and frightened out of her life, and terribly miserable. And honestly nobody can ever do much good if they are scared and unhappy."

"Lucy is always for giving the under-dog a chance!" said Pat, giving Lucy a warm hug. "You're a good sort, Lucy, old thing. You're quite right, of course."

And so it came about that Erica was not seen again at St. Clare's, except once by Lucy who went to say good-bye to her. That was two days later when Erica was up again, looking pale and unhappy. She was glad to be going away – but dreaded all that her mother would say.

"Now you just tell your mother honestly that you've been a mean and spiteful girl!" said Lucy. "And tell her you know it and you're going to start all over again and be just the opposite. You can, you know! Write to me next term and tell me how you're getting on."

So poor, mean little Erica disappeared from St. Clare's to start again somewhere else. Nobody missed her, and nobody waved to her as she went down the school drive in a taxi with her trunks. She had made her own punishment, which is always much harder to bear than any other.

"How's Margery getting on?" Matron was asked a dozen times a day, and at last in despair she put up a bulletin on her door, which read: –

"Margery is getting on nicely."

"Golly! Just like royalty!" said Janet, when she saw the bulletin. "You know – when the king is ill they put a notice outside the gate about him."

Lucy and Pat were the first two allowed to see Margery. They brought flowers and grapes and went into the cosy little dressing-room, which was lighted by a dancing fire.

"Hallo, old girl!" said Pat, presenting the flowers. "How's the heroine?"

116

"Don't be an idiot!" said Margery. "Oh, what glorious daffodils! And oh, how did you know that my favourite grapes were those big purple ones!"

"Here's something from Isabel," said Pat, bringing out a jigsaw puzzle. "And Janet sent you this. Everybody's got something for you, but Matron won't allow too much at once."

Margery flushed with pleasure. She looked at the jigsaw from Isabel and the book from Janet. She forgot the pain in her leg in her delight at being spoilt like this.

"How's Erica?" she asked.

"She's gone," said Lucy. "She's not coming back again."

"Gone!" said Margery, startled. "Why? Is she ill?"

"No," said Lucy. "She's gone because she couldn't face the school now that they know it was she who ruined Pat's jumper and spoilt her books."

Margery stared in the utmost amazement. "But you said it was I who did those things," she said. "How did you find out it was Erica?"

Lucy told her. "And we all owe you a humble apology for being so unjust," she said. "Please accept it, Margery. We will make it up to you when you are out and about again."

Margery seldom cried, but the tears came shining into her eyes now. She blinked them away in shame. She did not know what to say for a minute.

"Well, I don't wonder you thought I was the one who did those spiteful things," she said at last. "I've been so awful. And it's perfectly true I've been expelled from about six schools for rudeness and sulkiness. But you see – nobody cares about me at home – and so I'm miserable, and I'm always badly-behaved when I'm miserable."

117

"Don't tell us if you don't want to," said Lucy. "But if it's going to help – *do* tell us. We'll understand, you may be sure."

"Well – there's nothing much to tell, really, I suppose," said Margery, looking into Lucy's friendly eyes. "It's probably my own silly fault. You see – my mother died when I was little. She was such a darling. And my father married again and my step-mother didn't like me. She said awful things about me to my father and he ticked me off like anything. I – I loved him awfully – I still do, of course. I'd give anything in the world to make him have a good opinion of me. He's so marvellous."

Margery stopped and bit her lip. The others said nothing.

"My stepmother had three boys, and my father was terribly pleased. He always wanted boys. So I was pushed into the background and made to feel I wasn't wanted. And of course I got worse and worse and more and more unbearable, I suppose. I gave me stepmother a bad time, I was so rude and hateful. And that made my father angry. So I'm the black sheep of the family, and I just got to feel I didn't care about anything at all."

"And so you were sent to boarding-school and went on being unpleasant there," said Lucy, taking Margery's big strong hand in her little one. "Oh, Margery – I'm terribly sorry. You haven't had a chance."

"But won't your father be awfully bucked when he hears how you rescued Erica!" cried Pat.

"I shan't tell him," said Margery. "He won't know. He wouldn't believe it if anyone did tell him! He thinks I'm no use at all. You know, he's wonderful – so brave and courageous. He climbed Mount Everest.

"Golly!" cried Pat, in astonishment. "I say, he

118

must be marvellous – and you take after him, don't you? You are so strong, and so good at games and gym – and so frightfully brave too."

Margery's eyes suddenly lighted up. She lay looking up at Pat as if Pat had said something simply miraculous.

"I never, never thought of that before," she said. "But I believe I *do* take after him! It's lovely to think that. Yes – I'm awfully strong – and I suppose I *am* brave too, though that's not much to my credit really, because strong people ought always to be brave. Oh, you made my happy by saying that, Pat. I think my father would think a lot more of me if he knew I was like him!"

Matron came in as the conversation reached this interesting point. She was pleased to see Margery's happy face. "You've done her good," she said. "But you must go now. My word, what lovely flowers! Tell Isabel that she and Janet can come tomorrow, Lucy."

The two of them said good-bye and went out. Pat caught hold of Lucy's arm as soon as they were outside the door. Her eyes were bright.

"Lucy! Oh, Lucy! I've got a most marvellous idea."

"What?" asked Lucy.

"Listen!" said Pat. "You know that there's a picture of Margery in the local paper, don't you – and a long bit telling all about how she saved Erica? Well – I'm going to cut that out and send it to Margery's father – with a letter telling all about her and how very proud we are of her at St. Clare's!"

"I say – that really *is* a good idea!" said Lucy. "I wish I'd thought of it. We can get the address from Miss Theobald. My word – that will make Margery's father sit up a bit – to think that St. Clare's is so proud of her! That will will be a bit different from the opinion of the other schools she's been to. Well – it's time Margery had a bit of luck. I expect it was partly her own fault she didn't get on with her stepmother, because she *is* difficult – but the treatment she had at home only turned her from bad to worse. How silly some parents are! When I think of my own – so kind and understanding – I feel jolly sorry for Margery."

After this long speech the two girls said nothing till they reached the common room. Then Pat took the local paper and snipped out the paragraph about "Brave Schoolgirl Heroine" with Margery's picture.

"What are you doing?" asked Isabel, curiously.

"I'll tell *you* but no one else," said Pat. So she told Isabel, and she and her twin and Lucy set to work to compose the letter to Margery's father.

Here it is, just as it was written by the three of them.

DEAR MR. FENWORTHY,

We know that you are a very brave man, because Margery has told us about you. Perhaps you have heard how brave Margery is too, though you may not have been told all the details. Well, here they are.

Margery climbed up an iron pipe to the window-sill of a burning room, and rescued a girl called Erica. She tore sheets into strips and tied them to the bed. She climbed down them with Erica over her shoulder. She fell from the ladder and broke her leg and hurt her head. She saved Erica's life, and is a real heroine.

Margery is awfully strong. You should see her at gym, and she is almost the best in the school already at games. She won the last match for St. Clare's. We

think that she must take after you, because we are quite
sure she is already strong and courageous enough to
climb mountains or anything like that. She is getting
a bit better now, but we think she is rather lonely, so
it would be lovely if you had enough time to spare to
come and see her.

We are all as proud of her as we can be, and we hope
she will stay at St. Clare's till she leaves school alto-
gether. We thought you ought to know all this so that
you could be proud of her too.

With kind regards from three of Margery's friends.

PAT and ISABEL O'SULLIVAN, and LUCY ORIELL.

The girls were quite pleased with this letter, and they
posted it off the same day. It had an immediate effect
– for the next day Margery had a telegram that excited her very much. It was from her father.

"Very, very proud of you. Coming to see you today.
Love from Daddy."

Margery showed the telegram to Isabel and told her
to tell Pat and Lucy. "I'm so happy," she kept saying.
"I'm so awfully happy. Fancy my father sparing the
time to come and see me. He's proud of me too! It's
simply marvellous!"

The girls watched eagerly for Margery's father to
arrive. He was a fine-looking man, tall, broad-shoul-
dered and good-looking. He was very like Margery.

He was shown into Miss Theobald's room, and then taken to Margery.

What happened between Margery and her father nobody ever knew for certain, for Margery guarded her precious secret jealously. She could not even tell Lucy of those wonderful minutes when her father had taken her into his arms and praised her and loved her. Everything had come right. She had at last what she wanted and had missed so much, and in a few short minutes all that was best in Margery's character came up to the surface – and stayed there.

"Pat – Isabel – Lucy – you wrote to my father!" said Margery, next day, her eyes shining brightly. "He showed me your letter. You're dears, all of you. It's made all the difference in the world! He didn't know a bit what I was like – and now he does – and he's terribly pleased to know I am so exactly like him! I'm going mountaineering with him next hols.! Think of that! And he's going to let me stay on at St. Clare's, and then, when I'm eighteen. I'm to go to a training college to train to be a games-mistress. I've always wanted to do that."

"Margery – you do look different!" said Pat, marvelling at the glow in Margery's good-looking face. All the sullenness was gone.

"I'll be able to work well and happily now," said Margery. "I shan't be at the bottom of the form any more!"

"No – you'll be shot up into the top form, I expect, and send for us poor first-formers to make your tea and clean your boots!" laughed Lucy. "Don't you get too swollen-headed, my girl! You'll hear about it from Janet, if you do!"

Margery was allowed to hop about on one leg fairly soon, with crutches. Although she had to miss games and gym she didn't fret at all. Nothing seemed to matter to her now, she was so contented and happy. She worked well, and the mistress began to like this new, cheerful Margery.

Lucy and she made firm friends. Margery could not do enough for the merry, friendly Lucy, who only came up to her friend's shoulder. They were always together, and it was good to hear them joking and laughing.

"Lucy ought always to be happy," said Pat, as she watched her helping Margery down the passage with her crutches. "There's something simply lovely about her – she's one of those people you just can't help liking."

"Well, there's no reason why she shouldn't be happy," said Isabel. "She's got a lovely mother – and a famous father – and she's very clever and pretty. She just loves St. Clare's too. She told me yesterday that she means to be its head-girl someday. I bet she will too."

But ill-fortune came swiftly to poor Lucy the next week. A telegram came to Miss Theobald and Lucy was sent for out of the history class. She went to the Head Mistress's study, feeling rather frightened. What was the matter?

Miss Theobald was looking grave. She held out her hand to Lucy as the girl came in, and drew her to her.

"Lucy," she said, "I have some rather bad news for you. Can you be brave?"

Pat and Isabel helped Margery along

"Yes," said Lucy, her lip trembling. "Tell me quickly."

"Your father has been in a motor accident," said Miss Theobald. "He is badly hurt. He wants you to go to him."

"He won't – die – will he?" said Lucy, her face very white.

"I hope not," said Miss Theobald. "Go and ask one of the girls to help you to pack a small bag, and then I will take you to the station. I'm sorry, my dear – but things may not be so bad as they appear. Be brave."

Lucy hurried off and asked Margery to help her. The bigger girl was unhappy to see Lucy so upset. She put her arm round her and hugged her. "Cheer up," she said. "You may find things are all right. I'll pack your bag for you. Just you tell me what you want to take."

Very soon poor white-faced Lucy was driving to the station with Miss Theobald. The first-formers were sad and subdued, and Margery missed her friend terribly. It seemed all wrong that anything like this should happen to merry, friendly Lucy.

"I'm going to pray hard for Lucy's father," said Janet. "As hard as I can."

All the girls did the same, and thought a great deal of Lucy and wondered what was happening. Margery had a letter in four or five days. She told the others what it said.

"Lucy's father is out of danger," she said. "But an awful thing has happened to him. He'll never be able to use his right hand properly again – and he's a painter!"

The girls listened in dismay. "It's terribly hard luck on him," said Margery, "and hard luck on Lucy too –

because if he can't make money by his portrait-painting, there won't be any! So Lucy won't be able to stay on at St. Clare's."

"What a shame!" cried Tessie. "She's the nicest girl that ever came here!'"

"And she had planned to be head-girl one day," said Pat. "Oh gosh – what bad luck! Poor old Lucy. She must be so terribly upset about her father – and then to see all her future changed in a moment like that – it must be terrible."

"She'll have to leave school and take a job, I suppose," said Hilary. "St. Clare's is expensive. What a pity she can't win a scholarship or something."

"She could if she was in the third form," said Tessie. "There's a scholarship set there, sitting for an exam. at the end of next term – and the winner has the right to go to one of a dozen special schools, free of fees."

"But Lucy is only in the first form," said Pat. "Oh dear – I wish something could be done. Margery, is she coming back this term at all?"

"Yes, when her father leaves the nursing home in two days' time," said Margery, looking at the letter. "We mustn't be all over her when she comes back. That would only upset her. Let's be quite ordinary and friendly. She'll know we are feeling for her all right."

Lucy got a great welcome when she came back. She was pale and her face had gone thin, but she held her head up and smiled her old sweet smile. She could be as brave in her way, as Margery!

The girls did not say too much to her, and Margery took her off to show her what the class had done during the week she had been away. Lucy took her friend's arm and squeezed it.

"You're so nice to me, Margery," she said. "Thank you. You sent me a lovely letter. It did help. Poor

126

Daddy – you can't think how brave he is. He knows he will probably never be able to paint again – but he means to try with his left hand. He's so brave. He blames himself teribly now because he never saved any money – so Mummy and I have got hardly any. You see, he always made as much as he wanted to – and spent it all! We none of us bothered about saving. We thought Daddy could always get as much as he wanted."

"Will you really have to leave St. Clare's after this term?" asked Margery.

"Of course," said Lucy. "We couldn't possibly afford the fees. If I could only have stayed on I might have won a scholarship to some other school. As it is I'm going to leave and Mummy is looking out for some sort of a job for me. I'm quite quick, you know, and I could learn to be a secretary, I'm sure."

"I shall miss you dreadfully," said Margery. "Just as I've got a friend for the first time in my life! Oh, I wish I could do something about it!"

Margery was not a person to sit down lightly under misfortune, and she puzzled and puzzled about how she might do something to help Lucy. And then she suddenly got an idea. If only, only it would work! She told nobody about it at all, not even Lucy, but went straight to Miss Theobald.

The Head Mistress had some one with her. She called out "Come in!" when Margery knocked, and the girl went in. Her good-looking face was bright with her idea, and Miss Theobald marvelled to see the difference in her looks.

"Oh, Miss Theobald – I didn't know you had any one with you," said Margery, in disappointment. "I did want to ask you something very badly."

Miss Walker, the art mistress, was there. She had

been talking to the Head Mistress and had not yet finished. Miss Theobald looked at Margery and saw her eagerness.

"What do you want to speak to me about?" she asked. "Is it anything private?"

"Well – yes, it is rather," said Margery. "It's about Lucy."

"How strange!" said Miss Theobald. "Miss Walker has also been speaking to me about Lucy. Well – I think you can say what you want to with Miss Walker here. You know that she is very interested in Lucy, because she is so good at art."

"Miss Theobald – you know Lucy is going to leave after this term, don't you?" said Margery. "Well, she is awfully unhappy about it, because she does love St. Clare's – and she is exactly the sort of girl you want, isn't she? We all love her. Well, Miss Theobald, I've got an idea."

"And what is that?" asked the Head, trying not to smile as Margery almost fell over her words in her eagerness to get them out.

"Miss Theobald, you do think Lucy is awfully clever, don't you?" said Margery. "She's always top of our form, and she's got the most wonderful memory. Why, she's only just got to *look* at a page and she knows it by heart!"

"That's a gift," said Miss Theobald. "I know Lucy has it. She is very lucky. Well – go on, Margery."

"Don't you think Lucy is clever enough to sit for the scholarship exam. with the third form next term?" said Margery, her eyes shining. "I'm sure she'd win it, because she'd work so awfully hard! Couldn't you give her a chance to do that, Miss Theobald? She's worth it, honestly she is."

"You needn't tell me that," said Miss Theobald.

128

"We all know that Lucy is worth helping. I would keep her on at St. Clare's at reduced fees – but her parents will not hear of that. But, Margery, my dear – Lucy is only fourteen – and all the other girls going in for the exam. are sixteen. I know she's clever – but I doubt if she is as clever as that. It would only mean a great deal of very hard work – and probably a bitter disappointment at the end. There are one or two clever girls in the third form, you know."

Margery looked dismayed. She had set her heart on her idea. She had felt so certain that Lucy was clever enough to win any scholarship, if only she had a few months to prepare for it!

Miss Walker joined in the conversation. "I don't quite see how going in for the scholarship exam. will help Lucy to stay on at St. Clare's!" she said.

"Oh, but Miss Walker, it *will*!" cried Margery. "I've looked at the list of schools that are open to scholarship girls free of fees – and St. Clare's is one of them this year! So of course Lucy would choose St. Clare's, if she won the scholarship."

Miss Theobald began to laugh. Margery was so very determined about it all. "Really, the running of this school is being taken out of my hands!" she said. "What with Lucy deciding what was to be done about Erica – and writing that letter to your father, Margery – and now you telling me how we can manage to keep Lucy on – I feel a Head Mistress is not really needed at St. Clare's."

"Oh, Miss Theobald, we all know that it's you that makes the school what it is," said Margery, going red. "But you've no idea how popular Lucy is, and how we all want to keep her. She's the first friend I've ever had – and I've been puzzling my brains how to help her. I did think this idea might be some good."

"Well, Margery, I don't somehow think it will work," said Miss Theobald. "I'm not going to overwork a brilliant brain like Lucy's, two years below the scholarship exam. age unless there is a very great hope of her winning it. Miss Walker has also been to me with ideas about Lucy – and we have been talking them over."

"Oh, how nice of you, Miss Walker!" said Margery, who had never very much liked the art-mistress before – entirely her own fault, for she had never tried at all in Miss Walker's excellent classes! Now she felt that she would do anything for Miss Walker because she had taken an interest in Lucy.

"Well, my idea was that we should try to keep Lucy here for a couple of years somehow – and then let her go in for an art scholarship," said Miss Walker. "Her art is so brilliant already, that she is bound to be an artist of some sort. She must go to the best art-school in the country – but she is too young yet. I didn't somehow feel I wanted her to go in for shorthand and typing and get a job as a junior clerk somewhere, when she could make such good use of her time here – and then win a place at a London art-school."

"I've already offered to let Lucy stay here at reduced fees for two years, so that she might try for an art scholarship then," said Miss Theobald, "but her parents will not hear of it – neither will Lucy either, Margery, though I don't suppose she has told you that. She apparently wants to do her bit in helping to keep her family now that her father can't paint."

"Miss Theobald – couldn't you keep Lucy just one more term and let her try for the scholarship?" said Margery, eagerly. "Then she could be here for two or three years if she won it – and then try for an art scholarship. She'd get that easily enough!"

130

"Well, Margery, we'll see what can be done," said Miss Theobald. "It's certainly an idea I hadn't thought of – and I'm still not sure it can possibly be carried out. I shall have to talk to other mistresses and find out more about Lucy's capabilities. I'll tell you as soon as we have decided something. In the meantime – thank you, my dear, for trying to be so helpful. I am more glad than I can say that you came to St. Clare's. We have helped you, I know – and now you are going to help us tremendously."

And A Little Good Luck Too

Margery left the drawing-room on her crutches, her face bright with hope. Surely, surely, something would be arranged for Lucy now! She did not say a word to anyone about what she had suggested, least of all to Lucy, in case nothing came of it.

"I know Miss Theobald will keep her word and look into the idea thoroughly," thought Margery, as she looked across the classroom at Lucy's rather sad little face. Lucy was brave – but she could not help feeling sad now. Things looked so different. All her bright future was gone.

Miss Theobald kept her word. She called a meeting of the first-, second- and third-form mistresses, and of Mam'zelle and Miss Lewis, the history teacher, too. She told them shortly what Margery had suggested.

They talked the matter out thoroughly. All the teachers liked Lucy Oriell and admired her quick brain and wonderful memory. Miss Lewis said at once that she could coach Lucy for the history section of the exam., and she was certain that Lucy would excel in that, whatever she did in other subjects.

"And her French is already perfect!" said Mam-'zelle. "She has spent many of her holidays in France, and she speaks French almost as well as I do!"

Mathematics were Lucy's weak point. She did not like them and found them difficult, though even here her quick brain helped her over difficulties. But mathematics were Miss Theobald's speciality. She was a wonderful teacher where they were concerned.

"I could give her special coaching there," she said. "The child is worth extra trouble. I know I do no coaching now, because the running of the school takes all my time – but I would make an exception for Lucy Oriell."

The meeting ended after an hour and the mistresses went to their various rooms. Margery, who knew that the mistresses had been summoned to Miss Theobald's room, wondered and wondered if they had been talking about Lucy. She soon knew, for Miss Theobald sent for her.

"Well, Margery," said the Head, coming to the point at once. "We've been discussing Lucy's future – and we think you are right – we think it *is* possible that she might win the scholarship. So I have written to her parents and put the idea before them. We must see what they say."

The answer came by telephone the next day. Mrs. Oriell had been delighted with the Head's suggestion. She knew how very much Lucy had wanted to stay on at St. Clare's – and if there really was a chance that the girl could win a scholarship and stay there without the payment of fees, going on to an art-school afterwards, then she should certainly be given the chance. "I'm so glad you think that, Mrs. Oriell," said Miss

Theobald, pleased. "Thank you for letting me know so soon. I will tell Lucy tonight."

Miss Theobald sent for Lucy and in a few words told her what was suggested. The girl listened with shining eyes. It all seemed too good to be true, after her terrible disappointment and shock.

"Oh, Miss Theobald – thank you very very much!" she said. "I'll do my best, I promise. I'll work terribly hard – all the holidays too. I'll win that scholarship somehow, and stay on here. It nearly broke my heart to think I'd have to leave just when I was so happy!"

"Well, that's settled then," said Miss Theobald. "I have discussed the whole thing with the other mistresses, and they are going to give you special coaching. I shall take you for maths. myself, and we must begin this very week, for every day's work will count. I will draw up a special time-table for you, because you will be taking different classes now. You must not be foolish and work *too* hard, though! I think I must tell Margery Fenworthy to keep an eye on you and make you take a rest when you get over-tired!"

"Oh – won't Margery be pleased!" cried Lucy, thinking of her friend with pleasure. "I shall tell her first of all."

"Yes – she will be delighted," said Miss Theobald. "Go and find her now."

Lucy rushed off and found Margery in the common room with one or two others. She pounced on her friend and made her jump.

"Margery! Listen! I've got the most marvellous news!" she cried. "You won't believe it! I'm staying on at St. Clare's!"

"Oh *Lucy*! Are you going to be allowed to go in for the scholarship exam. then?" cried Margery, wishing her leg was better, so that she might dance around.

"Why, Margery – what do *you* know about it?" said Lucy, in astonishment.

"Because it was all my idea!" said Margery, happily. "I thought of it. I went to Miss Theobald about it. But I couldn't say a word to you till I knew it was decided, in case you might be disappointed. Oh, Lucy – I'm so terribly pleased!"

"What a friend you are!" said Lucy, wonderingly, as she looked into Margery's strong, determined face. "How lucky I am to have you! Fancy you going to all that trouble for me. Oh, Margery, I'll never never forget this. I'll remember your kindness all my life long."

"Don't be silly," said Margery. "I'm the lucky one, not you! Why, now I shall have you here at St. Clare's with me, instead of being all alone. The only thing is – you will have to work so terribly hard. I shall have to keep my eye on you and see that you get some fun sometimes!"

"How funny – that's just what Miss Theobald said!" said Lucy, laughing. "Well, with the mistresses looking after my work and you looking after my play, I should be all right, shouldn't I?"

"What's the matter?" cried Pat, from her corner of the room. "What are you two talking about in such excitement? Has one of you got a 'Very Good' from Mam'zelle?"

"Not likely, these days!" said Margery. It was quite a joke that Mam'zelle never gave any one a Very Good now. "No – the excitement is – that Lucy is staying on here after all – and going in ˆr the third-form scholarship exam. at the end of next term. What about *that*?"

All the girls came over to say how glad they were. Lucy was happy again. It was lovely to be liked so much. It was lovely to have a friend who would do so much for her. If only her father's poor hand would get right, she would be even happier than she had been before the accident.

"Lucy," said Margery, that night, just before they went up to bed. "I've thought of something."

"Gracious – not another idea so soon!" said Lucy, teasingly.

"Yes – but about me, this time, not you," said Margery, rather soberly. "You know, I'm sixteen, and I've no right to be so low down in the school. It's only because I've never been able to settle for long in any school, so my education has been sort of hotchpotch, all mixed-up. But my brains aren't too bad if only I'll use them. Well, I'm going to use them like anything now – so that I can go up in form, and keep with you a bit. I couldn't bear to be in the first form whilst you forged ahead and became one of the top-formers, although you are two years younger. It's so difficult to be friends, proper friends, if we are in different forms."

"Oh, Margery – that would be splendid!" said Lucy at once. "Yes – I suppose I shall go up next term, and keep up in a higher form, if I *do* win that scholarship – and it would be lovely if you got put up too. Do work hard!"

And so, to every mistress's enormous astonishment, Margery Fenworthy, the dunce of the first form, suddenly produced excellent brains, and worked so much harder that one week she actually tied for top place with Lucy.

"Miracles will never cease!" said Miss Roberts, when she read out the marks to the form. "Margery, you'll be in the second form before you know where you are! Good gracious, what a surprise this is. Doris, perhaps *you* will give me a nice surprise next. You have been bottom for three weeks. What about trying for top place with Lucy and Margery next week?"

Every one laughed, Doris too. The first form was a very pleasant place to be in those last few weeks of term.

Janet is up to Tricks Again

It was Mam'zelle who seemed to spoil things each day. She had always had a very hot temper – but nowadays she seemed to be unusually irritable, and the girls felt the rough edge of her tongue in every lesson.

Janet got tired of it. She was very hot-tempered herself, and she found it difficult to control herself when Mam'zelle made some specially biting remark.

"Ah, Janet! Once more you have made the same mistake that you have made at least one hundred times this term!" said Mam'zelle one day, scoring a sentence with a blue pencil, and pressing so hard that it almost tore the page. "I have no pleasure in teaching a stupid careless girl like you."

"Well, I've no pleasure in being taught!" muttered Janet, angrily. She said it half under her breath, but Mam'zelle caught enough of it to look up with flashing eyes.

"*Que dites-vous?*" she cried. "What is that you said? You will please repeat it."

The class listened breathlessly. Mam'zelle was in one of her rages. That was exciting – providing it was some one else who was getting into trouble!

Janet was bold enough to repeat what she had said, and she said it loudly, so that all the class could hear.

"I said 'I've no pleasure in being taught!'" she repeated.

136

"*Méchante fille!*" cried Mam'zelle. "What has happened to all you girls this term? You are rude and careless and sulky."

The class knew that it was really Mam'zelle's fault, not theirs. She was so bad-tempered. They looked mutinous, and said nothing. Even Lucy would not look at Mam'zelle when her eyes flashed round the class.

"Janet, you will learn the whole French poem in this book, and you will write it out for me three times!" said Mam'zelle, her voice trembling with rage. The class gasped. The poem was three pages long!

"Oh, Mam'zelle!" said Janet, startled. "You know I can't do that. It would take me ages and ages. Besides, I'm not good at learning French poetry. It's as much as I can do to learn eight lines – and there must be about a hundred in that poem."

"Then it will make you think twice before you are rude to me again," said Mam'zelle. She took up her spectacle case and put her glasses on her big nose. Her face was flushed an angry red, and her head was aching. Ah, these English girls! They were terrible! How was it she had liked them so much before? She could not bear them now.

After the class Janet talked angrily about her punishment. "It's not fair," she said. "It's all Mam'zelle's own fault, the wretch! Can't she see that we won't stand her sarcastic remarks when we don't deserve them? I'm sure we work just as hard as we did last term – and look at Lucy, how good she is in French, and yet Mam'zelle scolded her like anything yesterday."

"Wasn't she always as bad-tempered as this then?" asked Lucy, in wonder.

"Gracious no," said Janet. "This is the fourth term I've been in the first form – and Mam'zelle has always been quite a brick before – well, she always did have a hot temper – but she wasn't *bad*-tempered, like she is now."

"Janet, I'll copy out that poem once for you," said Kathleen. "My writing is a bit like yours. Mam'zelle won't know. You can't possible do it three times yourself today."

"Oh, thanks, Kath, you're a brick," said Janet. "That *will* be a help. I wouldn't let anyone take on a part of my punishments if I could help it. But goodness me, Mam'zelle must be mad if she thinks I've enough time to do all she said!"

Kathleen copied out the poem once in Janet's French book. Sheila did it once too, for her writing was not unlike Janet's. Janet scribbled it out the third time and, with much trouble and pains, learnt it by heart. The whole class was sick of the poem by the time that Janet had it perfect.

She went to Mam'zelle at seven o'clock to take the written work and to say the poem. She said it in a sulky voice and would not look at the French teacher at all. By this time Mam'zelle had recovered a little and was half-sorry she had given the girl such a long punishment. But Janet would not smile at Mam'zelle, and would not even say good night to her when she went from the room.

"Ah, these impolite English girls!" said Mam'zelle, with a sigh. "They should go to school in France – then they would know what good behaviour and hard work are!"

Janet did not forgive Mam'zelle for her hardness. She was a dreadful girl for playing tricks and practical jokes, and had got into great trouble the term before for throwing fireworks into the classroom fire. She had not done anything very bad this term – but now she was determined to make Mam'zelle "sit up", as she called it, the last two or three weeks of term.

She told the others. "If Mam'zelle thinks she can treat me like that without my getting a bit of my own back, she's jolly well mistaken!" said Janet. "I'm going to pay her out – so look out for some fun!"

The class was pleasantly excited. They knew Janet's tricks and appreciated them, for Janet was clever and original with her jokes. What would she be up to now?

"You know, it was terribly funny last term when she threw the fireworks into the fire," said Pat to Margery and Lucy. "We really meant to play that joke on Miss Kennedy, a timid sort of mistress who took Miss Lewis's place for history last term. Well, Miss Roberts came along just when Janet had thrown about fifty in – and golly, we had fireworks from Miss Roberts then too, I can tell you!"

"I wonder what Janet will do?" said Doris, hugging herself, for she adored a joke, and was pretty good herself at playing them. "I've got a funny trick my cousin gave me at Christmas – it's a thing that looks exactly like spilt ink!"

"Oh, why haven't you shown it to us?" cried Janet, in delight. "I know the thing you mean – it's awfully good. Have you got it?"

"Well, I brought it to school meaning to give somebody a shock with it," said Doris, "but I couldn't find it. It must be somewhere about."

"Go and look, Doris. Go and look now," begged Pat, giggling. "Look where you haven't looked before. In your tuck-box for instance. You haven't opened that since the beginning of the term, when we ate everything."

The joke *was* in the neglected tuck-box! Doris pounced on it with glee. It was a thing which, when put down flat on a book looked exactly like a big,

139

irregular, shiny ink-blot – almost as if the ink-pot had been spilt.

Janet took it in delight. "This is fine!" she said. "Lend it to me, there's a sport!"

"Rather!" said Doris. "What will you do with it?"

"Wait and see, tomorrow," said Janet. So the class waited impatiently till French lessons came, and Mam'zelle bustled in, out of breath as usual.

It was French dictation that morning. Mam'zelle looked round the class, which was suspiciously good and docile all of a sudden.

"Take down *dictée*," she said. "Get out your exercise books, and begin."

Every girl had to take her book to Mam'zelle to be corrected after *dictée*. Janet took hers up when her turn came and laid it flat on the desk. Mam'zelle took up her fountain pen – and then, before her eyes, there appeared on Janet's perfectly clean book, a very large and shiny ink-blot!

"Oh, Mam'zelle!" cried Janet, in a doleful voice. "Look what you've done on my book! It must have been your fountain pen! Is it leaking? Oh, and I did try so hard with my *dictée* this morning!"

Mam'zelle stared in horror at the enormous blot. She couldn't believe her eyes.

"Janet! What can have happened!" she cried. She looked at her fountain pen. It seemed all right. And yet there was the tremendous blot, right across Janet's neat book.

"I'll go and blot it, Mam'zelle," said Janet, and took her book away carefully, as if she were trying not to let the blot run across the page. The class saw it clearly and buried their heads in their hands or under their desks to stifle their giggles.

Janet slipped the trick-blot into her pocket and then

Mam'zelle stared in horror at the enormous ink blot

pretended to be very busy with blotting-paper. Mam'zelle was shaking her pen with a puzzled air. She simply could not imagine how so much ink had run out of it so suddenly.

Janet took back her book, which was now absolutely clean. Mam'zelle stared at it in the greatest amazement.

"But where is the smudge?" she asked in astonishment. "You cannot have cleaned it so well!"

"Well, I've got some special blotting-paper, Mam'zelle," said Janet, in a solemn voice. "It cleans ink like magic."

"Ah, but it is indeed magic!" said Mam'zelle, pleased. "You *dictée* is now not spoilt at all. Thank you, *ma chère* Janet! I was so sorry to have spoilt your work."

One or two muffled giggles could be heard from Doris and Kathleen. Mam'zelle looked up sharply.

"There is nothing to laugh at," she said. *"Taisez-vous!"*

But, of course there *was* something to laugh at – and when Janet cleverly managed to slip the ink-blot on to Doris's desk, just as Mam'zelle was leaning over to look at her work, the class nearly had hysterics!

"Oh, Mam'zelle – that wretched pen of yours!" said Doris, in a reproachful voice, looking at the blot. "It's messed up my desk now."

Mam'zelle stared at it in surprise and horror. Blots seemed to be following her round this morning. She looked at her fountain pen again and shook it violently. A shower of ink-drops flew over the floor. Doris cried out loudly.

"It *is* your pen! Look at all the blots it has made on the floor! Oh, Mam'zelle, please may I borrow Janet's wonderful blotting-paper to wipe up the mess?

142

Miss Roberts will be so angry with me if she sees it there next lesson."

"I cannot understand it," murmured poor Mam'zelle, feeling she must be in some sort of a dream, as she looked at the large and shiny blot on Doris's desk. "I have never made such blots before."

The class went off into giggles that spread round uncontrollably. Mam'zelle lost her temper.

"Is it so funny that I make blots?" she cried. "Silence! Another giggle and I will keep the whole class in for break."

That was enough to keep the class quiet for a while, though there were many handkerchiefs stuffed into mouths when the urge to laugh became too great. Janet was pleased with the success of her joke, and already she was planning another.

"I'm going to put beetles into Mam'zelle's spectacle case," she giggled to the others, when they were in the common room after tea, discussing with enjoyment the success of the ink-blot. The second-formers had enjoyed the tale immensely and had groaned because they hadn't been able to share in the joke.

"Janet! Not *beetles*!" shuddered Sheila. "How could you possibly pick them up to put them in?"

"And anyway, how are you going to get them there?" said Pat.

"Easy enough," said Janet. "Mam'zelle is always leaving her spectacle case around. The first time she leaves it in our class-room I'll grab it and put the beetles into the case! What ho for a squeal from Mam'zelle! That will teach her to make me learn her horrid French poems!"

The very next day Mam'zelle left her glasses in their case on the first-form desk. Janet winked at the others.

She saw them at once. Immediately Mam'zelle was out of the room on her way to the second-form Janet whipped out of her seat and took the case from the desk. She slipped it into her pocket and got back to her seat just as Miss Roberts came in to take arithmetic.

The lesson had hardly been going for more than four minutes when a girl from the second form came in.

"Please, Miss Roberts, Mam'zelle is sorry to interrupt you, but may she have her glasses? She left them in a case on your desk."

Miss Roberts looked round the big desk and then opened it. No spectacle case was to be seen, which was not surprising considering that it was safely in Janet's pocket.

"It doesn't seem to be here," said Miss Roberts. "Mam'zelle will probably find that they are in her pocket."

The class giggled to itself. They knew quite well that Mam'zelle would find nothing of the sort! Janet looked quite solemn. It made the others giggle to look at her.

"Girls! What is the joke, please?" asked Miss Roberts, impatiently. She did not like giggles. "Is there anything funny in Mam'zelle losing her glasses?"

As it happened, there was – but Miss Roberts, of course, didn't know it. The class sobered down.

"Well, Miss Roberts, it's only that Mam'zelle is *always* leaving her glasses about," said Doris.

"Quite," said Miss Roberts, drily. "Turn to page forty-seven, please. KATHLEEN! If you stare round the class any more I'll put you with your back to it! What *is* the matter with you this morning?"

The class had to behave itself. Miss Roberts made it work so hard that most of them thought no more of the next trick Janet was going to play, until break came. Then they all crowded round Janet to see her put the poor surprised beetles into the spectacle case!

Mam'zelle Gets Another Shock

Janet collected various kinds of beetles and grubs from underneath fences at break. Giggling loudly the first- and second-formers watched her take out Mam'zelle's spectacles and carefully put in the wriggling insects. They were half-dazed with their winter sleep. Janet shut the case with a snap.

"I hope the beetles can breathe," said Kathleen, in a troubled voice. She was passionately fond of animals, and her kindness extended even to spiders, beetles and moths.

"Of course they can breathe," said Janet. "This spectacle case is as big as a room to them!"

"What are you going to do with the case?" asked Hilary. "Are you going to put it back on the desk so that Mam'zelle can open it next day?"

"Of course, silly," said Janet. "We all want to see the fun, don't we?"

"I say, Janet – won't Mam'zelle be absolutely furious?" said Lucy. "She'll tell Miss Theobald, I should think. Better be careful – you don't want to get into a fearful row just before the end of term. You might get a bad report."

"I don't care," said Janet. "I'm going to get even with Mam'zelle, the bad-tempered thing!"

The beetles and grubs passed quite a pleasant time in the spectacle case, and didn't seem to mind at all, though Kathleen kept worrying about them and opening the case to give them a little air. In the morning Janet placed the case on Miss Roberts's desk just before Mam'zelle came to give her daily French lesson. The whole class was in a state of fidget and excitement. They had tried to keep it under whilst Miss Roberts was teaching them, for she was very clever at sensing anything wrong with the class.

She had been rather sharp with them, but had not seemed to suspect anything. She left to go to the second-form – and Mam'zelle came in. Mam'zelle had had a bad night. She was not sleeping well these days, and her eyes were circled with big black rings.

"Bon jour!" she said, as she came in. She went to the desk, and put down her books. The girls wished her good morning and sat down. Mam'zelle turned to the blackboard and wrote down a few questions which the class had to answer in writing, in French.

Then suddenly Mam'zelle spotted her spectacle case. She pounced on it with delight.

"Ah! Here are my glasses! Now this is a strange thing! I sent to ask for them yesterday and was told they were not here! All day long I looked for them!"

The girls watched in the most intense excitement. The ones at the back craned their necks round the girls in front of them, trying their hardest to see. The girls at the front were thrilled to have such a good view.

Mam'zelle sat down. She did not open the case at once. She looked round the class. *"Dépechez-vous!"* she cried. "Why are you so slow at beginning your work today!"

The class took up their pens. Mam'zelle yawned and tapped her big white teeth with her pencil. Why, oh why didn't she open her spectacle case?

Ah! Now she was going to. She stretched out her

146

hand and picked up the case. She opened it slowly — and out scrambled the quick-legged beetles, and out crawled the grubs, wide awake now because of the warmth of the room!

Mam'zelle stared at them. She took out her handkerchief and rubbed it across her eyes. Then she looked cautiously at the spectacle case again. She simply could not believe her eyes.

"It is impossible!" thought poor Mam'zelle. "My eyes tell me that there are beetles and grubs crawling over my desk, but my sense tells me that my glasses should be there. And no doubt they *are* there. It is because I am tired that I see these insects crawling out of my case!"

The girls were trying to smother their giggles. Mam'zelle's face was so funny! It was quite plain that she was immensely astonished and couldn't believe her eyes.

Mam'zelle was trying to think calmly. She hated anything that crawled, and one of her favourite nightmares was that beetles were crawling over her. And now here they were walking out of her spectacle case. It was quite impossible. Beetles did not live in spectacle cases. Her eyes must be wrong. She must go to the occulist again and get fresh glasses. Perhaps that was why she had such head-aches lately! All these thoughts passed through poor Mam'zelle's mind, and the first formers peered over their books and watched eagerly to see what would happen.

"It cannot be that these insects are real," Mam'zelle was thinking firmly to herself. "They are in my imagination only! My glasses must be in the case, although it appears to me that there are insects there instead. I must be brave and put my hand into the case to get my glasses. Then, when they are safely on my

147

nose I shall see that the beetles are not really there!"

The girls began to giggle, though they tried their hardest to stop. Mam'zelle was so puzzled and so amazed. It did not seem to enter her mind for one moment that it was a trick. She put out her hand to feel for the glasses she felt sure must really be in her case.

And, of course, all she got hold of were beetles and grubs! When she felt them in her fingers she gave a loud scream. The girls watched in enjoyment. This was simply marvellous!

"What's the matter, Mam'zelle?" asked Doris, demurely, winking round at the others.

"Ah, Doris – Janet – come up here and tell me what there is on my desk," said poor Mam'zelle, looking down in horror as one beetle ran round and round the ink-pot and finally fell right into it.

Doris and Janet leapt up at once. Janet stared solemnly at Mam'zelle. "Your glasses are in your case," said the naughty girl. "Put them on, Mam'zelle, and maybe you will see properly."

"My glasses are not there!" cried Mam'zelle. "But do you not see those insects, girls!"

"What insects?" asked Doris, innocently, and the whole class exploded into stifled giggles. But Mam'zelle hardly noticed them.

"Ah, there is something wrong with me!" she groaned. "I have feared it all these weeks. I am not the same. My temper is so bad. I am so irritable. And now my eyes are wrong. I see things! I see beetles on this desk! If only I could find my glasses!"

Janet picked up the empty case, quickly slipped Mam'zelle's glasses into it, from her pocket, and then took them out of the case as if they had been there all the time. She handed them to the astonished French mistress.

"Ah, this is worse than ever!" cried Mam'zelle. "So they were there all the time and I could not even see them! And alas, alas – still the beetles they crawl over my desk! I am ill! I must leave you! You will go on with your French quietly, please, and wait till Miss Roberts comes back. I am ill – *très malade, très malade!*"

Mam'zelle left the room stooping like an old woman. The class were startled and dismayed. This was not the right ending for a joke at all! Mam'zelle had taken it really seriously. She had believed Janet and Doris when they had assured her that the insects were not there. The girls stared at one another in dismay. Janet picked the insects off the desk and put them carefully out of the window.

"Janet, I don't like this," said Lucy, in her clear voice. "We've given Mam'zelle a real shock. It sounded to me as if she hadn't been feeling well for ages and thought that our joke was all part of her illness. I wish we hadn't done it now."

Everyone wished the same. Nobody giggled. Janet wished that Mam'zelle had seen through the joke and had punished her. This was much worse than any punishment. The girls took up their pens and got on with their work, each feeling decidedly uncomfortable.

In about ten minutes Miss Theobald came in. The girls stood up at once. The Head Mistress glanced at the board and at the girls' books. She saw that they were working and she was pleased.

"Girls," she said, in her low, pleasant voice, "I am sorry to tell you that Mam'zelle is sure she is ill, so she will not come back to you this morning. I have sent for the doctor. Please get on with what work you can, and wait until Miss Roberts returns."

She went out. The girls sat down. They felt more uncomfortable than ever. Janet was very red. She kicked herself for playing such a trick now. She thought about Mam'zelle and her bad temper. Could it have been because she was feeling ill?

The first form were so subdued that morning that Miss Roberts was quite astonished. She kept looking at the bent heads and wondering what was the matter. But nobody told her.

At the end of the morning there was a regular buzz of talk in the common room. "Did you know that Mam'zelle is very ill? Whose form was she in when she was taken ill? Oh, yours, Margery? What happened? Did she faint or something?"

Nobody gave Janet away. They all felt that she was sorry about the trick, and they were ashamed too – so they said nothing about the joke at all. It had gone very wrong and goodness knows how it could be put right.

Mam'zelle was put to bed, and Matron went to see to her. Poor Mam'zelle was more worried about her eyes than about anything else. She kept telling Matron about the insects she had seen, and she declared she was afraid to go to sleep in case her nightmare came back.

Janet went to ask Matron how Mam'zelle was after tea. The doctor had been, so Matron was able to tell the girl all the news.

"It's overwork and strain," she told Janet. "Poor Mam'zelle's sister was ill all the Christmas holidays and she went to nurse her. She nursed her day and night, and got very little rest or sleep herself. So she came back tired out, and instead of taking things easy, she worked herself all the harder. I know you girls thought her very bad-tempered and irritable this term – but that's the explanation!"

"Did she – did she say anything about her spectacle case?" asked Janet.

Matron stared at Janet in surprise. "What do *you* know about her spectacle case?" she said. "As a matter of fact something seems to be worrying poor Mam'zelle terribly. She keeps saying that her eyes are going wrong because she saw insects coming out of her spectacle case – and she daren't go to sleep and get the rest she needs because she is so afraid she will dream that insects are crawling over her. She is in a very over-tired state!"

Janet went away to tell the others. So that was the explanation of Mam'zelle's bad temper that term! She had been nursing her sister day and night – and, knowing Mam'zelle's zeal and thoroughness, Janet could well imagine that she had spared herself nothing in the holidays. Mam'zelle had the kindest heart in the world, in spite of her hot temper.

"I do feel simply awful about that trick," said Janet to Pat. "I really do. I've a good mind to go into Mam'zelle's room and tell her about it to set her mind at rest. I simply daren't tell Miss Roberts or Miss Theobald."

"Well, go and tell Mam'zelle then," said Pat.

"That's a good idea. Take her some flowers from me. And some from Isabel too."

Every girl in the class put money towards flowers for Mam'zelle. As the next day was Saturday they were able to go down into the town to buy them. They bought daffodils, narcissi, anemones and primroses. They all felt so guilty that they spent far more money than they could really afford.

Miss Roberts saw the girls coming back with their flowers, and stared in amazement.

"What's this – a flower-show?" she asked.

151

"They're for Mam'zelle," said Hilary, which astonished Miss Roberts all the more, for she had heard the bitter complaints of her form about the amount of work set by Mam'zelle that term, and her bad temper when it was not done properly.

"These first-formers have really kind hearts," thought Miss Roberts. She spoke aloud to them. "This is very nice of you. Mam'zelle will be pleased. She had a very bad night, so I don't expect any of you will be allowed to see her. But you can take the flowers to Matron to give to her."

But that wasn't Janet's plan at all! She was going to see Mam'zelle somehow, whatever Matron said!

Last Week of Term

Pat and Isabel kept watch for Matron after tea that day. They were to tell Janet when she was not about so that Janet might slip in by herself. Janet was not going to take the flowers in with her. They were outside the room in a cupboard and Janet meant to go and fetch them as a kind of peace-offering when she had confessed everything to Mam'zelle.

Poor Janet was rather white. She didn't at all like the idea of facing Mam'zelle, even when she was ill. But it had to be done. Pat and Isabel saw Matron come out of Mam'zelle's bedroom with her tea-tray and they went to her.

"Matron, please may we have a clean towel?"

"What have you done with yours?" asked Matron, bustling along with the tray. "Come along and get it then, I haven't much time."

Pat looked back over her shoulder and winked at

Janet to tell her that Matron wouldn't be back for a few minutes. The twins meant to keep her talking and give Janet a clear field.

Janet slipped to Mam'zelle's door. She knocked and a voice said *"Entrez!"* Janet went in. Mam'zelle was lying in bed, looking up at the ceiling. She looked very unhappy, because she was still worrying about what was suddenly and mysteriously the matter with her eyes. She expected to see insects crawling all over the ceiling. Poor Mam'zelle – she would not have thought these things if she had not been so overworked.

She looked with surprise at Janet. Matron had told her there were to be no visitors that day.

"Mam'zelle," said Janet, going to the bed. "Are you better? I had to come and see you. I wanted to tell you something."

"It is nice to see you, *ma chére* Janet!" said Mam-'zelle, who was always touched by any kindness. "What have you to tell me, *ma petite*?"

"Mam'zelle – Mam'zelle – I don't know how to tell you," said Janet, "you'll be so angry. But please believe me when I say I'm terribly sorry – so are we all – and we wouldn't have done it if we'd know you'd been feeling ill – and . . ."

"My dear child, what are you trying to say?" asked Mam'zelle, in the utmost astonishment. "What is this terrible thing you have done?"

"Mam'zelle – we – I – I put those beetles and things into your spectacle case to pay you out for punishing me the other day," blurted out Janet, desperately. "And I put a trick ink-blot on my book too. You see . . ."

Mam'zelle looked at Janet as if she couldn't believe her ears. "Those – those crawling insects were *real*, then?" she said, at last.

153

"Yes, Mam'zelle," said Janet. "Quite real. I got them from places under the fence. I – I didn't think you'd believe it was your eyes that were wrong. Now you're ill we feel awful."

Mam'zelle lay quite still. So her eyes and her mind were quite all right. Those insects were not in her imagination, they were real. It was only a joke! If she had been well and quite herself she would have guessed that! But she was tired and could not think properly. How thankful she was that Janet and told her!

She turned to speak to the girl but Janet was not there. She had slipped out to get the flowers. She came back with her arms full of them, and Mam'zelle gasped to see them.

"Mam'zelle, these are from all of us in the first form," said Janet. "We are sorry you're ill – and please forgive us, won't you? Honestly we'd have put up with all your rages and everything if we'd known you were so tired!"

"Come here," said Mam'zelle, and reached out a large hand to Janet. The girl took it shyly. "I have been *abominable* this term!" said Mam'zelle, a smile coming over her face. "*Insupportable and abominable!* You will please tell the O'Sullivan twins that, Janet. I know the nickname they had for me last term – Mam'zelle Abominable, which they gave me because I said so often that their work was abominable! But this term I have really earned that name."

"You were awfully cross with us lots of times," said Janet, honestly. "But we don't mind NOW. We understand."

"Ah, you English girls! There is nobody like you when you are nice!" said Mam'zelle, quite forgetting all the dreadful things she had thought and said about them that term. "You will give my love to the others,

Janet – and my best thanks for these beautiful flowers – and you will tell them that if they will forgive me I will forgive them also – and you too, of course! *Méchante fille!* Wicked girl. Ah – but how brave and good of you to come and tell me!"

Janet stared at Mam'zelle and Mam'zelle looked at Janet with her big dark eyes. She began to laugh, for she had a great sense of humour at times.

"To think you put those beetles there – and I did not know it was a trick – and that ink-blot! What bad children you are! But how it makes me laugh now!"

And Mam'zelle went off in a loud burst of laughter. Matron was passing by the door at that moment and heard it in amazement. Thinking that Mam'zelle must have gone mad for a minute, Matron quickly opened the door and went in. She looked in astonishment when she saw the masses of flowers – and Janet!

"Janet! What are you doing in here? You naughty girl! I didn't give you permission to come. Go at once."

"No, Matron, I will not have Janet sent away," said Mam'zelle, most surprisingly. "She stays here to put my flowers in water! She has brought me good news. I feel better already. She makes me laugh, this *méchante fille.*"

Mam'zelle certainly looked better. Matron looked at her and then nodded to Janet that she might stay and put the flowers in water. Janet swiftly arranged them as well as she could. Mam'zelle watched her.

"The lovely flowers!" she said, contentedly. "Matron, do you see what beautiful bunches the girls have sent to their bad-tempered, insupportable old Mam'zelle?"

"I see them," said Matron. "Now, Janet, you must go. And if you come here again without permission I shall spank you!"

Janet went, with a grin. She ran straight to the common room to tell the others all that had happened. How glad they were to know that Mam'zelle had been such a brick about it all – and had actually laughed.

"Perhaps things will be better this last week of term," said Doris, who had suffered very much that term from Mam'zelle's rough tongue. "If Mam'zelle is well enough to come back for a few days at the end of term she'll be nicer – and if she doesn't I shall be jolly glad to miss French."

"This term *has* gone quickly!" said Pat. "It seems no time at all since half-term – and here we are almost at the Easter hols. What a lot has happened this term – almost as much as last term."

"More," said Isabel. "We didn't have a fire this term – or a heroine either!"

Margery blushed. She was getting very clever at using her crutches, and her leg was mending marvellously. Lucy twinkled at her.

"It always makes Margery go red if you say the word 'heroine'!" she said. "Pat, Margery is coming to stay with me for a week of the hols. We shan't have any maids or anything, because we are poor now, but Margery's going to help in the house all she can – isn't she a brick? I shall be working hard most of the time, but I shall take time off to be with Margery too."

"And then I'm going on a holiday with my father," said Margery. "What are you twins doing for the hols.?"

Holidays were certainly in the air. Every one was making plans for Easter. Some were going shopping to get new clothes. Alison was full of this, of course.

"Vain little creature!" said Pat, pulling Alison's pretty hair teasingly. "Well, you're coming to stay with us part of the hols. and you can bring your new pretties to show us – but we'll only allow you to boast *once* about them. After that – not a word!"

"All right, Pat," said Allison, who was really learning to be much more sensible. "I'll have one good glorious boast – and then be the strong silent girl!"

"You couldn't be silent!" said Isabel, who now liked her silly little cousin very much better. "If your own tongue couldn't talk, the tongues of your shoes would do it for you!"

The last week of term was very happy. Mam'zelle got much better, and the girls went into her room to see her and play a game with her. She was the same old jolly Mam'zelle she used to be, now that she had had a rest, and had changed her ideas about "these English girls". She was already making plans for next term's work – but the girls refused to listen!

Lucy had been working hard to prepare for the scholarship exam. next term. She had had good news of her father and this made her work with much more zest and happiness. Miss Theobald and the other teachers had worked out her holiday tasks and praised her for the progress she had already made. So Lucy looked much happier, and laughed and joked like her old self.

The twins were happy too. Things had gone well that term. They were top in five subjects. Lucy did not go in for the class exams. as she was doing so much extra work, or she would, of course, have been top in everything except maths. Doris and Alison were bottom in most things, but they were both quite cheerful about it.

"Somebody's got to be bottom," said Doris to Alison, "and I think it's rather sweet of us to be willing to take such a back seat in everything!"

"Willing! You jolly well can't help it, you duffer!"

said Pat. "But who cares? You can make us laugh more than anybody else in the form – so you go on being bottom, old girl!"

The last day came, and the excitement of packing and saying good-byes. Mam'zelle was up once more, making jokes and writing down everyone's address. There was laughter everywhere, and occasionally Miss Roberts's voice was lifted in complaint.

"Kathleen! Is it necessary to yell like that? Sheila, you don't look at all elegant rolling on the floor to do your packing. PAT! PAT! Stop pummelling Janet. What a bear-garden! I shall set you all a hundred lines to write out in the train home and send me tomorrow!"

There were giggles and squeals at this. It was fun to be going home – fun to look forward to Easter and Easter eggs, to long walks through the primrose woods, and reunions with dogs and cats and horses at home, to say nothing of mothers and fathers and little sisters and brothers.

"See you next term!" called Pat. "Don't forget to write, Janet. Be good, Doris! Oh, Isabel, don't drag me like that – I'm coming! We're off in the first coach, everybody! Good bye! See you all next term!"

Yes – see you all next term. That's what *we* will hope to do – see them all next term!

THE ENID BLYTON TRUST FOR CHILDREN

We hope you have enjoyed the adventures of the children in this book. Please think for a moment about those children who are too ill to do the exciting things you and your friends do.

Help them by sending a donation, large or small, to the ENID BLYTON TRUST FOR CHILDREN. The trust will use all your gifts to help children who are sick or handicapped and need to be made happy and comfortable.

Please send your postal orders or cheques to:

The Enid Blyton Trust For Children,
International House
1 St Katharine's Way
London E1 9UN

Thank you very much for your help.